Hurricane

L. RON HUBBARD

Hurricane

Published by
Galaxy Press, LLC
7051 Hollywood Boulevard, Suite 200
Hollywood, CA 90028

Printed in the United States of America.

ISBN-10 1-59212-284-1
ISBN-13 978-1-59212-284-4

Library of Congress Control Number: 2007903533

Contents

Stories from Pulp Fiction's Golden Age

A ND it *was* a golden age. The 1930s and 1940s were a vibrant, seminal time for a gigantic audience of eager readers, probably the largest per capita audience of readers in American history. The magazine racks were chock-full of publications with ragged trims, garish cover art, cheap brown pulp paper, low cover prices—and the most excitement you could hold in your hands.

"Pulp" magazines, named for their rough-cut, pulpwood paper, were a vehicle for more amazing tales than Scheherazade could have told in a million and one nights. Set apart from higher-class "slick" magazines, printed on fancy glossy paper with quality artwork and superior production values, the pulps were for the "rest of us," adventure story after adventure story for people who liked to *read*. Pulp fiction authors were no-holds-barred entertainers—real storytellers. They were more interested in a thrilling plot twist, a horrific villain or a white-knuckle adventure than they were in lavish prose or convoluted metaphors.

The sheer volume of tales released during this wondrous golden age remains unmatched in any other period of literary history—hundreds of thousands of published stories in over nine hundred different magazines. Some titles lasted only an issue or two; many magazines succumbed to paper shortages during World War II, while others endured for decades yet. Pulp fiction remains as a treasure trove of stories you can read, stories you can love, stories you can remember. The stories were driven by plot and character, with grand heroes, terrible villains, beautiful damsels (often in distress), diabolical plots, amazing places, breathless romances. The readers wanted to be taken beyond the mundane, to live adventures far removed from their ordinary lives—and the pulps rarely failed to deliver.

In that regard, pulp fiction stands in the tradition of all memorable literature. For as history has shown, good stories are much more than fancy prose. William Shakespeare, Charles Dickens, Jules Verne, Alexandre Dumas—many of the greatest literary figures wrote their fiction for the readers, not simply literary colleagues and academic admirers. And writers for pulp magazines were no exception. These publications reached an audience that dwarfed the circulations of today's short story magazines. Issues of the pulps were scooped up and read by over thirty million avid readers each month.

Because pulp fiction writers were often paid no more than a cent a word, they had to become prolific or starve. They also had to write aggressively. As Richard Kyle, publisher and editor of *Argosy*, the first and most long-lived of the pulps, so pointedly explained: "The pulp magazine writers, the best of them, worked for markets that did not write for critics or attempt to satisfy timid advertisers. Not having to answer to anyone other than their readers, they wrote about human beings on the edges of the unknown, in those new lands the future would explore. They wrote for what we would become, not for what we had already been."

Some of the more lasting names that graced the pulps include H. P. Lovecraft, Edgar Rice Burroughs, Robert E. Howard, Max Brand, Louis L'Amour, Elmore Leonard, Dashiell Hammett, Raymond Chandler, Erle Stanley Gardner, John D. MacDonald, Ray Bradbury, Isaac Asimov, Robert Heinlein—and, of course, L. Ron Hubbard.

In a word, he was among the most prolific and popular writers of the era. He was also the most enduring—hence this series—and certainly among the most legendary. It all began only months after he first tried his hand at fiction, with L. Ron Hubbard tales appearing in *Thrilling Adventures, Argosy, Five-Novels Monthly, Detective Fiction Weekly, Top-Notch, Texas Ranger, War Birds, Western Stories,* even *Romantic Range.* He could write on any subject, in any genre, from jungle explorers to deep-sea divers, from G-men and gangsters, cowboys and flying aces to mountain climbers, hard-boiled detectives and spies. But he really began to shine when he turned his talent to science fiction and fantasy of which he authored nearly fifty novels or novelettes to forever change the shape of those genres.

Following in the tradition of such famed authors as Herman Melville, Mark Twain, Jack London and Ernest Hemingway, Ron Hubbard actually lived adventures that his own characters would have admired—as an ethnologist among primitive tribes, as prospector and engineer in hostile climes, as a captain of vessels on four oceans. He even wrote a series of articles for *Argosy,* called "Hell Job," in which he lived and told of the most dangerous professions a man could put his hand to.

Finally, and just for good measure, he was also an accomplished photographer, artist, filmmaker, musician and educator. But he was first and foremost a *writer,* and that's the L. Ron Hubbard we come to know through the pages of this volume.

This library of Stories from the Golden Age presents the best of L. Ron Hubbard's fiction from the heyday of storytelling, the Golden Age of the pulp magazines. In these eighty volumes, readers are treated to a full banquet of 153 stories, a kaleidoscope of tales representing every imaginable genre: science fiction, fantasy, western, mystery, thriller, horror, even romance—action of all kinds and in all places.

Because the pulps themselves were printed on such inexpensive paper with high acid content, issues were not meant to endure. As the years go by, the original issues of every pulp from *Argosy* through *Zeppelin Stories* continue crumbling into brittle, brown dust. This library preserves the L. Ron Hubbard tales from that era, presented with a distinctive look that brings back the nostalgic flavor of those times.

L. Ron Hubbard's Stories from the Golden Age has something for every taste, every reader. These tales will return you to a time when fiction was good clean entertainment and the most fun a kid could have on a rainy afternoon or the best thing an adult could enjoy after a long day at work. Pick up a volume, and remember what reading is supposed to be all about. Remember curling up with a *great story*.

—Kevin J. Anderson

KEVIN J. ANDERSON *is the author of more than ninety critically acclaimed works of speculative fiction, including* The Saga of Seven Suns, *the continuation of the Dune Chronicles with Brian Herbert, and his* New York Times *bestselling novelization of* L. Ron Hubbard's Ai! Pedrito!

Hurricane

CHAPTER ONE

The Convict

H E came through the rain-buffeted darkness, slipping silently along a wall, avoiding the triangular patches of light. His stealth was second nature because he had lived with stealth so long. And who knew but what death walked with him into the leaden gusts which swept through the streets of Fort-de-France, Martinique?

He was big, heavy boned, and he had once weighed more than he did. His eyes were silver gray, almost luminous in the night like a wolf's. His black hair was plastered down on his forehead, his shirt was dark, soggy with the tempest, and at his waist there gleamed a giant brass buckle. Capless and gaunt, feeling his way through the sullen city, he heard voices issuing from behind a door.

He stopped and then, indecisively, studied the entrance. Finally he rapped. A moment later a dark, fat face appeared in the lighted crack.

"*Qu'est-ce que c'est?*"

"I want food. Food and perhaps information."

"The police have forbidden us to open so late. Do you wish to cause my arrest?"

"I have money."

The doors opened wider. The mestizo closed and bolted

3

the double door. A half a dozen men looked up, curiously, and then returned to their rum punch.

"Your name is Henri," said the tall one, standing in a puddle of water which oozed out away from his shoes.

Henri raised his brows and rubbed his hands, looking up and down the tall one's height. "You know my name? And I know you. You are the one they call Captain Spar."

"Yes, that's it. Then you got the letter?"

"Yes, I received the letter. I do not often associate with . . . convicts."

Captain Spar made no move. "I have money."

"How much?"

"One hundred dollars."

Henri waved his fat hands. "It is not enough. There are police!"

"I have one hundred dollars, that's all."

"I expose no risk for a hundred dollars. Am I a fool? Go quickly before I call the gendarmes."

"I'll attend to getting out of here by myself. I want only food, perhaps some clothes."

Henri subsided. "But how did you come here?"

"Stowaway. The captain found me, allowed me to get ashore here, would carry me no further. Our friend wrote you in case that happened."

"He did not say that you would only have a hundred dollars. Let me tell you, young fellow, an American is conspicuous here on a black island. I run no risks for a paltry hundred dollars. If you are caught, you will be sent back and I will be

4

sent with you. I disclaim any interest in you or knowledge of you. If you want food, I will serve it to you as a customer. That is all."

Henri waddled away, his neck sticking like a stump out of his collarless white-and-blue striped, sweat-stained shirt. Henri was greasy to a fault, thought Captain Spar. Slippery, in fact.

Presently Henri came back, bringing the makings of a rum punch—syrup, *rhum vieux*, limes and a bowl of cracked ice. Captain Spar made his own drink and as he sipped it, he said, "Would you know of a man here who calls himself the Saint?"

Henri shook his head. "Who is that? Can it be that you actually came back into French territory, risking your neck, to find a man?"

"Perhaps."

"Perhaps for some of that hundred—"

"If your information is right, you get paid."

"Tell me what you know of this man, first. Tell me why you want him."

Captain Spar looked over the glass rim and then nodded. "All right. You know my name. That's my right name, strangely enough. One time, not five years ago, it was a very respected thing, but now . . .

"Five years ago I was in Paramaribo, temporarily out of a job. I was approached by a ship's broker who said that a man who called himself the Saint was in need of a captain. I had not heard of the Saint, but it was said that his headquarters were Martinique.

5

"The job was simple enough. I was to sail for New York in command of a two-thousand-ton tub of rust. The loading had already been done, so they said. All I had to do was get aboard and shove off.

"Just as I was about to sail, men swarmed down upon the ship, boarded us, announced that they were police, and began to search. In a few minutes they had dragged a dozen men from the hold. They turned all of us over to the French authorities who immediately sent us down to French Guiana.

"I was accused of trying to aid penal colony convicts to escape, and with a somewhat rare humor, they determined that I should join the men they thought my comrades at their labor in the swamps.

"That was five years ago. Two weeks ago I made my way to the sea, found this friend of mine, recovered the money he had been keeping for me, stowed on a freighter, and here I am in Martinique. I want the Saint."

Henri nodded thoughtfully. "Yes, there is a Saint here."

Captain Spar sat forward, his sunken eyes lighting up with a swift ferocity. "Here? Where?"

"I can tell you all about it," said Henri, "but I do not want money for my efforts. Oh, no, *m'sieu*. You can do me a small favor, and then perhaps I shall tell you all about the Saint, where he can be found, how you can kill him."

"Name the favor," said Spar.

"Two blocks down, on the left of the governor's house, you will find a small café. Go there tonight, now. Wait there in a room at the back. Soon there will be men asking for you. Give them a package I have made ready. That is all."

"Sounds easy," said Spar, thinking of nothing but the Saint. "Where is the package?"

Henri went out and returned presently with a small, light box. Spar put it in his shirt, eased through the door and went down the shining wet streets, keeping close to the walls.

His thoughts were not very nice. For five years he had cherished them, nursed them, lived with them, until now he was living for only one thing. He wanted to get the man who had sent him there. Wanted the pleasure of feeling that man die between his hands.

It was not a nice thought. But in the penal camps of French Guiana, neither are things nice. The fever, the labor, the privation, all leave a bitter stamp. Swollen jungle rivers, back-and-heart-breaking labor. Sun and storm. And fever. And guards. And the association of damned men to drive one who has been civilized to the verge of insanity.

Once Spar had been a merchant captain of steady reputation, but all that had faded from him now. He stalked like a black panther through the rain, merging with the shadows, on the lookout for the shine of a badge, dreading recapture only because it would mean forswearing the vengeance he hoped to wreak on the Saint.

He found the small tavern without any difficulty. It stood drearily in the blackness, flush with the street, overshadowed by a balcony. Standing beside the open gutter which ran torrents, Spar regarded the structure, wondering whether or not he was walking into a trap. But trap or no, if it led to one who called himself the Saint, Spar was ready for it.

He went in, cautiously. A big man in a white apron seemed

to be expecting him. Without a word, Spar was led over the rough boards back through the taproom and into a small, isolated cubbyhole beyond.

The place had the unfinished appearance of a piano box. Only one chair was there, and the back of that was toward the door.

Spar turned it around and sat with his back to the wall. One could never be too sure.

He did not sit at ease. He twisted about nervously, his fever-yellowed face forever turning from one to the other of the two doors. He started at small sounds. In the outer room, a mechanical piano was banging away with all its brass-gutted abandon. It was the first semblance of music Spar had heard in five years.

He became more jumpy as the time went on. And then he was suddenly calm. The presence of danger acted like a bromide upon him. The door had moved an eighth of an inch. No more. A gust of heavily odorous air whispered through the crack, making a low moaning sound.

An instant later the other door moved. No one came in sight. The wind moaned more loudly, dismally. The mechanical piano was still. The wash of the rain across the sheet-iron roof was heavy and dull at times, and then again would resemble the scampering of a thousand rat feet.

The tension became stiff. Slowly, Spar climbed to his feet and stood, leaning a little forward, waiting. He knew as well as though a voice had shouted that he was about to be killed.

Perhaps the Saint had already learned of his presence. Perhaps the Saint was striking first. Little by little the left-hand door swung back. All was darkness beyond it. The only light came from a feeble bulb in the ceiling of the unfinished room. Water roared down the eaves and the wind moaned again.

In that heavy, oppressive mustiness, Spar heard a shoe creak. In the same instant he dived for the left-hand door.

A revolver shot flaming sparks into the room. The bullet snapped through the timber over Spar's head, showering him with sparks and dust.

He slammed the door wide open. A heavy body was in his hands. He gripped the wrists. The revolver lashed up and down as though anxious to be free. His assailant was striving to smash out Spar's brains.

Spar hung on, rocking back and forth in the darkness. He heard running feet at his back, crossing the narrow room. He lashed out with his left fist, sent the man he held rocketing away from him. His right caught and held the revolver.

A shot barked behind him. Spar whirled to meet this new danger.

Henri!

Henri stopped and tried to take a careful aim, but his face blanched and his hand was shaking when he saw that he did not have the opportunity to shoot Spar in the back. Having missed the first time, Henri did not intend to miss the second.

They stood for a full second, facing each other across ten feet of space. Then Spar ducked to one side and brought up the recovered gun.

Henri's shot went wild. Spar fired with a chopping motion. Henri melted back, wilting. The gun drooped and slid out of stiffening fingers. But before he fell, Spar was conscious of a movement at his side.

His first antagonist, taking advantage of Spar's distraction, was holding a chair on high, ready to smash down on Spar's skull.

Spar rolled swiftly to one side and fired. The chair clattered harmlessly to the rough boards. The man stumbled and sprawled between the upturned legs, hands stretched out as though reaching for his escaping life.

But even then, Spar had no time to breathe. Footfalls came from the taproom and the door was opened by a tall, thick, black man who stood in the opening with a lordly air.

Spar was about to fire when the man raised his hand.

"No, let this be as it is. The dogs deserved it for their bungling. I am your friend."

The black man came in. He hauled the body away from the chair and sprawled it out beside Henri's crumpled form. Then he slapped his hands together after the fashion of Eastern monarchs and a moment later four men entered, bearing another body among them.

But this man was not dead. He was either drugged or drunk. The four threw him on the floor and stood back.

The big man flicked an imaginary speck from his starched white coat and looked at Spar. "I am Chacktar. Your identity does not concern me in the least. Henri said you were a convict, escaped from the colony. So much the better. I have a use for you. If you fail to carry out my orders, I shall turn you over to the French police here and you will go back. You do not want that, I know. Here, you men, bring this young fellow to."

*His first antagonist, taking advantage of
Spar's distraction, was holding a chair on high,
ready to smash down on Spar's skull.*

The four began to work on the drugged man and Spar studied the fellow. He was young, obviously an American. Blond hair streamed down over his face. His well-cut clothes were torn. But for all that, the face bore marks of long standing. The stamp of dissipation was there, the jaw was weak, the eyes heavily shadowed.

After a few minutes the young fellow came to, sitting up weakly, holding his head between his hands and staring through his knees at the floor.

"Now, *Monsieur* Perry," said Chacktar, "what have you to say for yourself?"

Perry shook his head as though to rid it of a fog. "Wha-What happened?"

Chacktar sent a meaning look at Spar. "You, *Monsieur* Perry, in your drunkenness killed these two poor, defenseless men. You know what that means. You'll hang!"

Perry crawled to his feet and stood weaving back and forth. "Me? I . . . I what?"

"You killed these men. A good thing it sobered you up. A drunken beast you are. What will your father say? And Miss Mannering. Ah, but we must get out of here. The police have heard your shots. They will be coming, instantly."

"I . . . I killed those . . . two?" stammered Perry.

"God take me!" bawled Chacktar. "Don't you know?"

"No, I don't . . . remember. Why did I do it?"

"Some quarrel. I happened in just as the last one struck you over the head with that chair."

Spar was about to intervene when he felt a gentle hand

take the revolver out of his fingers. One of the men had come up to his back. A round muzzle was pressing against his spine.

"This sailor," said Chacktar, "saw it all. Didn't you?"

Perry looked pleadingly at Spar. The pressure of the gun at Spar's back grew heavier. Spar thought about the penal camps. After all, he owed this youth nothing. And any present statement was worthless.

"Yes," said Spar.

Chacktar nodded. "Then we must go. Leave these two bodies here for the police. We must get young Perry back up to his house."

Urged along by the gun, Spar followed the black man and the boy, much perplexed.

CHAPTER TWO

Flight

THE house which belonged to the Perrys sat on a high hill, far back and far above Fort-de-France. When the party gained the summit by a back road, Spar looked down at the sparsely lit city and the church cross which stood out, gleaming in the rain. Somewhere in that town he would find the Saint. That was enough. He stumbled on through the mud, following Chacktar's black slicker.

They passed through hedges of red flowers, faint patches in the blackness, and finally ascended the steps of a mansion which had the air of quiet dignity.

A black servant let them in. Chacktar, with a serious urgency about him, strode on through the halls and pushed through a large door to a huge living room which was furnished in wicker and hanging draperies.

Six people were there, seated languidly in the comfortable chairs. They had the appearance of solid assurance, of wealth, of power.

Spar halted in the doorway, a sour grin twisting his mouth. This was a long way from the slime and slaving of the prison camp. A long way from French Guiana. But if he didn't watch his step, the way would not be so far.

A quiet gentleman with a gray beard and a sharp, handsome

face sat forward, glass in hand, staring at the group in sudden alarm. "What is this? Tom, what's this?"

The boy Perry he addressed, shuffled weakly forward, eyes down, dead white, fumbling with his hands. "Tell . . . tell him, Chacktar."

Chacktar made a great show of reluctance, and then squaring his shoulders and looking like a tower of ebony in his dripping slicker, he said, "Tom was very drunk, *Monsieur* Perry. In a fit of rage, he killed two men."

The entire group stood up, aghast. The elder Perry turned pale. "Tom, how could you? Killed . . . killed them? Where?"

"In a rum house, that's where!" snapped Tom, coming alive with a show of defiance, suddenly fighting as a rat fights when trapped. "You won't let a man get drunk decently. No, he's got to sneak off and do it on the sly. And what if I did kill a couple of—"

"Tom," said the elder Perry. "Come to, man, this is serious. They'll arrest you. And even the power of Frederick Perry won't keep you from the gallows."

"Frederick Perry." said Tom, derisively.

Chacktar led the boy into the next room at a sign from the elder man. Spar was left standing by the door, water running from his hair down over his shoulders and thence to his shoes. The big brass buckle sparkled unashamed.

"We must do something," moaned the elder Perry, standing up and walking down the room. "We must do something. We've got to get him away . . . tonight."

Spar looked at the others. He saw them at first as a general group and then one person stood out from them and the others were lost in a vague haze.

Spar stood up straighter, stared, without knowing that he stared. And the girl was staring at him, blue eyes alert and frank.

It had been a long while since Spar had seen a beautiful woman. Five years. And this girl was beautiful beyond any he had ever seen. Her hair was a silvery mass, matching the becoming pallor of her skin. Her figure was graceful. Her bearing was that of a princess. She was dressed in a blue dinner gown which matched her eyes, and her only jewels were a string of pearls which matched the soft whiteness of her throat.

Startled and suddenly ashamed of his stare, Spar dropped his eyes, as shaken as a man who had unwittingly set foot in Paradise. He felt dirty in that moment. Ragged and worthless. He was sorry he had come. Before he had not realized, but now . . .

"Yes," the girl said, looking away from Spar, "we must get him away." A weary note was in her voice and she moved her slender, well-kept hands in a helpless gesture.

Spar edged slowly toward the door, hoping that no one would notice him, but then Chacktar came back. "I've told him to pack, *Monsieur* Perry. Servants are at work even now."

A sullen-faced man who wore a jacket bearing four gold bands stepped belligerently forward. "But how can he go?"

"On the *Venture,* of course," said Perry.

"I am the captain of the *Venture,*" said the one in gold braid.

"What do you mean, Larson?" demanded Perry.

"That I carry no murderers while I work for you. And I have a contract. I cannot jeopardize my reputation for that worthless sot of yours."

"None of that," said Perry. "Do you mean you'd desert me now?"

"Call it that if you will."

Another gentleman moved forward to the two. He was small, dressed foppishly in a mess jacket, black sash, tuxedo pants. The tight-fitting, abbreviated white coat bore silver buttons. The fellow had a small mustache, a slender face, a dreamy dark eye.

"We make too much of this," he said.

"Not enough, Count Folston," replied Perry.

Count Folston smiled. "But certainly you can buy the officials out."

Perry scowled. "Hardly. I have the interests of Perry Sugar Central to consider. I have my own reputation to think about. I must get him away before anyone finds out."

"But," said Folston with a shrug, "that would only brand him what he is. I believe it would be better if the *Venture* set to sea with a yachting party."

"But I cannot go," said Perry. "I have my business."

A light but throaty voice floated out of the back of the room. "Oh, I think that would be just dandy."

Perry glared, Folston smiled.

Spar looked into the shadows to see a black-haired, jet-eyed girl who puffed slowly on a cigarette she held in a long holder.

She looked quite Spanish, very sophisticated. Spar instantly disliked her.

"Miss Bereau is right," said the girl in blue. "It would be better if we all went."

"Correct, Peg," said Folston. "It's your decision, seeing that someday you will be marrying the brute."

Spar's heart sagged within him. This dream married to that drunk? Impossible!

"Yes," said Folston, stifling a yawn with a dainty slap, "we had better all go. That will make it look better. A sea cruise is what we need. I myself am rather bored with Martinique. So little excitement here, you know."

The man with the gold braid bristled again. "I'm not taking anyone out on the *Venture*. There's a storm, and there's my ticket to consider. Do what you like with your boat, Perry. Count me out." He picked up his garish cap from the bookshelf, bowed to all those present, and stepped past Spar and out of the room.

"Obedient blighter," said Folston. "Is the mate fit to captain her?"

"The mate?" said Perry. "Oh, my God, I forgot the mate. He's in the hospital. He fell down a hatch and broke his leg."

"Then we have no captain," said Folston, pondering the matter, chin in hand.

"Can't . . . can't you get a captain?" said the girl in blue.

"No, Miss Mannering," said Perry. "Not here in Martinique."

Spar looked at them all. He wondered what they would say and do if they knew he was an escaped convict from the penal colony. Probably throw him to the official wolves, doubtless.

For minutes he had been debating about the Saint. Should he stay here and try for vengeance or come back later? Right now, penniless as he was, to stay might be very foolish. And then, he owed a debt to the girl in blue. She had made him realize that the world contained something other than death and fever and slime. She had been an excellent stabilizer for a man who has long lived in madness. A glimpse had been enough.

But he had better not trust these men, these women. Somehow, he would get free. Once more he started to edge toward the doorway. A flash of white eyeballs was there in the darkness of the foyer. A glint of steel. Spar stopped and again faced the room.

"This man," said Chacktar, "witnessed the killing."

For the first time, the others noticed Spar's presence. The girl in blue, Peg Mannering, frowned slightly and stared again.

"Humph," snorted Perry into his beard. "Well, how much do you want? Out with it! But I won't pay any great sum, you understand. Things could happen to you, you know."

Spar gave them his sour, twisted grin and suddenly felt superior to all of them. Rich, yes. Well dressed, well bred. But stained—all except the girl in blue, who would marry the drunken wastrel, Tom Perry.

Spar said, in a hard, rough voice, "Keep your money. There are still respectable men left in this world."

"He witnessed the shooting," said Chacktar again. "Didn't you, Captain?"

Spar was about to shake his head when he saw a bulge in Chacktar's pocket and remembered the man in the foyer. No use getting killed over such cattle of the Perrys.

"Sure," said Spar.

"Captain, did you say?" said Perry.

"Yes, what of it?"

"You have papers?" demanded Perry, coming near.

Spar grinned. When he had recovered his hundred dollars, he had also recovered his ticket. He pulled it out of his shirt and unwrapped the protecting oilskin from it, presented Perry with the engraved license which proclaimed Captain Spar a master mariner.

"Ah," said Perry.

Folston smiled and stifled another bored yawn. "That's luck, Perry. Come, children, we go to pack a yachting cap or two."

Peg Mannering did not seem to hear Folston. She was looking at Spar with a queerly intense expression. Finally she dropped her eyes and turned away, followed by the girl called Miss Bereau. As she passed, Miss Bereau threw Spar a ravishing smile.

"Now to terms," said Perry, when he and Spar were alone.

"Five hundred to New York," replied Spar.

"Good enough. You'll find clothes on the *Venture*. Take young Perry straight to New York and, above all things, keep him sober."

"Aye, aye, sir," said Spar, saluting with a mocking smile. "But it's a wet night to walk. Please call your car."

CHAPTER THREE

Hurricane

CAPTAIN SPAR alighted in the darkness by the small landing stage which Fort-de-France uses for its public wharf. To his left he could see the gleam of the granite war memorial, to his right he could see the single row of dingy taverns. The car drove away and left him alone in the rain.

He could see the lights of two ships in the anchorage. One he knew to be the freighter which had befriended him, the other must be the *Venture*. Their uneven paths of light came across to him, dull in the flurries of water and wind.

Several rowboats bobbed in against the wharf. Spar cast about for some minutes before he could find a boatman who would take him to the ship. Then he sat in the stern while the boatman pulled sleepily at the oars, and watched the white sides of the *Venture*.

The yacht was of considerable size. A Diesel-engined vessel of about a hundred and ten feet, a steel ocean charger glittering with wet brass and clean paint.

Spar gave the boatman two francs and went up the gangway to the deserted deck. Up to that moment he had felt lost and strange, but the contact of the planking with his soggy shoes gave him an almost electric shock.

How good it was to be in command again.

Some of the half-mad look went out of his silver gray eyes. Some of the slump went out of his shoulders. He clattered up the bridge ladder to the superstructure and entered a cabin.

The man with the four gold stripes was there, hastily throwing his dunnage into a locker trunk. He looked up with hostile glance when Spar entered and then went on packing.

"So they sent you," said the man with the gold stripes. "Well, sailor, you can take it from Dan Larson that you're up against a whole ocean full of trouble. Mind you," he added, throwing suits of whites into the top compartment, punctuating his speech with the slap of cloth, "I don't hold anything against you. I'm genuinely glad to be out of it with a whole skin."

"Why so?" said Spar.

"Aw, you don't know. You don't know. I took this job when I was on the beach. It seemed fine, being all dressed up and having nothing to do. But I learned different, believe me. Tonight—well, tonight the glass says that we're in for a hell of a blow. I wouldn't put out, myself, but you'll have to if Perry hired you. You'll weather it if you're good enough. If you're good enough. The crew is black and they haven't enough sense to be afraid. They'll obey you—if you're hard-boiled.

"But wait until you have Tom Perry on this tub. Just wait. He's an arrogant, besotted, worthless wastrel, that's what. Three sheets to the wind forever. He'll try to boss you and take command if you don't watch it."

"I've got my orders from Perry," said Spar.

"That won't help you. And if you don't watch Perry, the old man, you'll be swimming in boiling oil. He's ruthless.

How do you think he built up a central on Martinique if he isn't ruthless?"

"I don't know. The others are all coming with Perry."

Larson stopped, jaw slack. "That bunch? Good God, what have you got yourself into? They're no good. All except Miss Mannering. She's okay, though I don't see how she fits into the picture at all."

"Who is she?" said Spar.

"Daughter of Clyde Mannering, head of a rival central. Old man Perry is trying to squeeze old Mannering out and old Mannering thinks marrying his girl to young Perry will seal the bargain."

"Oh," said Spar, seeing light. "Have you any spare clothes?"

"I keep the slop chest under that leather seat. You'll find dungarees and so forth in there. It's all there is."

"Just so they're dry," said Spar. He kneeled down by the transom and pulled out several suits until he found one of the right size. To the pile he added a slicker and a cap. Then he stood up and removed his sopping shirt. He did so thoughtlessly, anxious to be rid of his wet clothes. He eyed the private shower which opened out from the big cabin and picked up the dry clothing.

But Larson had watched the movement and Larson had seen certain marks across Spar's great back which had been laid there with a whip. "So that's what you are," said Larson.

"What?" said Spar, startled, facing the former captain.

"I wondered why you were here, how you were at liberty to take the job. Hell, I never thought I'd get that low. Handing my job over to a *penal colony convict*."

25

"So what?" said Spar.

"Escaped convict," muttered Larson. "Well, jailbird, you're in good company. Murderers and God knows what else. I thought your face looked drawn. I thought you were too alert and watchful. What am I supposed to do?"

"Anything you like," said Spar, dropping the clothes and stepping forward.

"Do you think I'll keep this to myself?"

"I think you will," replied Spar.

Larson carelessly dropped his hand to his hip pocket. Spar stepped another pace ahead. "Don't pull it."

Larson jumped back, dragging at his gun. Spar struck with all the power of his arm. Larson dropped back against the transom, head limp, blood spurting from his torn cheek.

Spar dragged the man to his feet and knocked him down again. The madness had come back to his eyes. His mouth was twisted into an ugly grin. He reached again for Larson's jacket and then, with an effort, stood up straight.

"Get up," said Spar. "If you can't stand the idea of a man getting free from French Guiana and hell itself, run ashore and yap your news to the police. Now stand up and take this locker and get the hell out!"

Larson crawled to his feet, dazed. He shouldered his trunk and staggered with it out to the deck. A sailor came and took it from him, the pair went over the side, and the ship's tender spluttered away through the rain.

Spar stood breathing hard, fists still tight. A trickle of blood ran down his knuckles and dripped to the rug. Presently he picked up the clothes and went into the shower.

"Get up," said Spar. "If you can't stand the idea of a man getting free from French Guiana and hell itself, run ashore and yap your news to the police."

He found a razor and shaved and, looking into the mirror, he was startled at the worn, bitter lines of his face. At thirty he looked old. But then five years in French Guiana are not apt to give a man anything but bitter lines.

The Saint was responsible for every twist. The Saint had done that to him. And for a full minute, Spar was in the grip of fury. His impulse was to go ashore instantly, leave this chance for escape, and find that devil and kill him as he had promised himself for five years that he would do.

Then he remembered that Larson had preceded him ashore and the authorities would soon be out to investigate. He went on with his bath and finally dressed himself in the clean clothes.

The dungarees were not much of a uniform, but the brass buckle sparkled brazenly and the officer's cap was aslant over his lean, hard face. He looked capable.

He heard the return of the launch and presently footsteps on the deck below. Drawing on the slicker he went out with the rain hammering and stinging his face and found Folston coming up to the bridge.

"All here?" said Spar.

"Oh, rather," replied Folston. "Old Perry says to weigh away as soon as you can. Tom Perry is in his bunk and the girls are in the salon. Could we have something to eat, fellow?"

"Find the steward yourself," said Spar, annoyed by the overbearing tone of the man. "I'm here to run this hooker and you're here to ride in it. Get below and keep out of my sight."

"Oh, rather," said Folston. "Feel your authority, do you?

28

See here, my man, I'll have you understand that I am Count Folston and I have no intention whatever of—"

Spar lifted Count Folston off the ladder and to the lower deck. "There's the salon," said Spar. "Stay in it."

Folston glared and then shrugged. He went into the cabin and Spar continued aft to the engine room hatch. He swung down the maze of steel ladders until he came to the control platform.

A young white man was there, reading. He sat up when Spar approached. "Hello, who are you?"

"I'm Captain Spar, taking Larson's place. Get going. We go out in a few minutes."

"Out?" said the engineer. "Hell, man, it's blowing blazes and it'll blow harder before it blows less."

"Turn them over," said Spar and went above to the fo'c's'le. There he found several black sailors sitting sleepily about a dice game. They blinked at him.

"I'm your captain," said Spar. "On deck, the lot of you. Who's bosun here?"

"I am," said an aged, bulky black man.

"Then you're mate. Weigh anchor."

"Aye, aye, sir," said the new mate, puffing up with importance. "Look alive, you sons. Yes, sir, Captain sir, coming right up, sir."

Spar went back to the bridge. The deck was throbbing under his feet. The Diesels were going. A helmsman came and stood over the dim light of the binnacle. The anchor chain began to rasp up through the hawse.

Spar eyed the channel, the point to his port, the shoal buoys to his starboard, and slammed the telegraph down, up and down, to half speed ahead.

The *Venture* shook harder under the shove of the engines, the black rain-lashed sea parted before the bows, and they headed out.

Spar was grinning to himself. He felt better than he had felt for five years. The sensation of command, the feel of clean clothes. His lucky star was riding in the low black sky.

They successfully negotiated the channel and stood into the choppy whitecaps of the Caribbean. The compass swung to three hundred and thirty degrees and Spar jangled the engine room for another five knots. From the wing he could see the lights of the island.

"Well, my fine Saint," said Spar, "I'll be coming back in a short time. You'll know what hit you, never fear."

"What was that?" said a voice behind him.

Spar turned and stared into the blue eyes of Peg Mannering. "Oh, er, nothing. Better get below, miss, it's wet as all hell up here."

"Get below? Young Perry is getting drunk again. Can you do anything about it? You look . . . well . . ."

Spar smiled. "If you want me to, I'll try. But perhaps he'd be better off drunk in his cabin than bothering the deck."

"No, no. When he is drunk, he . . . Please do something about it, Captain. Mr. Perry gave you orders to that effect. Please."

"I can't leave the bridge this minute, but I'll be down shortly.

This blow is heavier out here in the open sea and we're still in close to land. Go below and I'll—"

"May I stay here, please?" said Peg Mannering.

"Why, certainly, if you don't mind the spray. If you wish, you can have my cabin."

Folston's mincing voice sounded at the top of the ladder. "Certainly you can have his cabin, Peg. Certainly. I'm sure our jailbird would love it."

Spar whirled about and faced the dapper count.

"Jailbird?" said Peg Mannering.

"Certainly, haven't you heard?" said Folston. "Larson told me when he came in from the ship. This fine convict knocked Larson's teeth down his throat and threw him down the gangway just because he found Larson packing in the cabin."

"If I were you," said Spar, stepping very close, "I would be very careful of what I said."

"Oh, I shall, I shall," said Folston in mock terror. "Pray don't frighten me, dear convict."

"Convict?" said Peg Mannering, groping along the rail, moving away from Spar.

"From French Guiana," said Folston. "Perhaps the French would like to see him. I believe he is very valuable down there in the labor camps."

"Devil's Island!" said Peg Mannering, nervously.

Spar glared at them both. "Yes, Devil's Island. Certainly. Why not? But right now, it so happens that you are on an American ship over which the French have no jurisdiction.

31

My papers have never been revoked, I am still a master mariner—and I still command the *Venture.*

"This ship may be the property of Frederick Perry and you may be all the kings and queens of the Continent. But right now you're passengers under my care.

"As for my right to be here, I've sailed these seas for years. I know them and they know me. And convict or no, the sea will let me pass. The sea isn't waiting on judgment from spoiled, pampered fools.

"As for your right here, you haven't any whatever. This sea is my sea, not yours. Look at it tonight. Swinging by and whipping at us, trying to drag us down. It's angry, but not at me. It's angry because you have no right here. It's trying to reach up and take you and drag you down into its blackness and swallow you up forever.

"Now get below."

Peg Mannering stared, afraid, at Spar and then looked down at the white-capped sea, whose waves looked like oily mountains topped with the teeth of spray.

"Get below," said Spar.

Folston smiled. "Very pretty, convict. Very pretty. We go because we don't exactly enjoy the stink of a prison camp. Come along, Peg."

But Peg Mannering stayed where she was and shook her head. "No. I'm afraid I would rather stand here than watch Tom Perry."

Folston shrugged. "There's no accounting for tastes," and disappeared down the hatch.

Spar turned his back on the girl and looked into the binnacle.

The helmsman, who had heard Folston's remarks, edged cautiously away. Spar gave him a scornful glance and went back to the wing.

Peg Mannering, slicker wrapped tightly about her slender figure, watched him. She had never seen a man like Captain Spar. He was so definite in his actions, so sure of himself now that he stood on a deck. She remembered how he had looked back in the drawing room of the Perry house.

He was handsome in his way. His eyes were odd, very light against the darkness of his face, and his skin showed the marks of fever, but something about the triangle of his eyes and mouth reassured her.

"It has been said," murmured Peg Mannering, "that a wolf is more to be trusted than a snake, however charming."

"Must I be a wolf?" said Spar.

"Aren't you?"

"No, I'm just a convict. Didn't you hear Folston? Who is that man?"

"He has great wealth, they say. He thinks he has enough to buy anything he wants."

"And you say he's wrong."

"Yes. Gold tarnishes in his hands."

Spar looked at her intently. "Just why are you going to marry Tom Perry?"

The direct shaft startled her. "That is out of my hands."

"But not out of mine," said Spar.

"What do you mean? You can't do anything."

"Oh, I know. I'm just a convict and I'll probably end up back in French Guiana. Larson will squeal, the New York immigration men will hold me, and I'll be shipped back. That's what happens when you fight the law. But right now..."

"You mean . . ." she backed away from him. "You mean you'd kill him?"

"No, nothing so crude. Convict, yes, but not a fool. If Tom Perry was removed, Folston would still be there. Folston has his eye on you. I know it. I can feel it. And your destination is not in your hands. Things haven't changed much since the slave markets of the Barbary Coast."

"You . . . take a great deal upon yourself."

"And why not? What do I lose? I know where I'm headed. I may get out of it, and if I do, I have business back in Martinique. But while I still breathe clean air and while I still keep away from swamps, I can do a few things. It won't make my lot any worse. I owe you a debt."

"Owe . . . *me?*"

"Yes. Before I saw you, I had nothing but death on my mind. You made me wake out of a five years' sleep. Just by looking at you, that's all. I owe you for that. Wolves can look at queens."

Piqued, but not knowing why, Peg Mannering stepped back from him. "And queens can order wolves shot. Don't forget that."

"I suppose so, Miss Mannering. I hope for his sake that Tom Perry—or Folston—can shoot quite straight and quite well."

He left her in the wing and went to the binnacle. Once more the helmsman drew away from him as though afraid, but Spar stood there, looking out through the spattered glass, watching the drive of rain across the decks.

In three hours, the blow began to pick up. They were well out into the Caribbean and received the full lash of the wind. The yacht was plunging her bows into the waves, and sometimes the bows stayed down for seconds at a time, shuddering. Then it would soar skyward again, rolling with a sick lurch and once more head down.

The deck was shifting under Spar's widespread feet, but he held to nothing. He seemed to be enjoying the storm, enjoying the clean ferocity of it.

From time to time, crashing sounds came from the main deck. Lashings were coming free and boats and rigging were giving way to crash through the darkness, reducing all to wet splinters in their path.

No sea is rougher or blacker or more spiteful than the Caribbean in a storm. The mother of hurricanes was fast building up the velocity of wind and the height of waves. Even now large vessels were going ashore in the hammered ports of the Antilles.

Sky and water met in the whirling embrace of blackness. Rain blotted out any light or gleam which remained. Combers raced across the decks, smashing into the masts and cabins and roaring back through the scuppers and into the sea.

The velocity of the wind had increased until it was impossible to hear anything below a shout. The Diesels throbbed, pounding against the waves.

Spar, aware though he was of their danger, grinned to

himself. He whistled down the speaking tube to the engine room and when answer came back, he said, "Half speed."

"It's about time," cried the harried engineer.

Spar looked back to the wing of the bridge. Peg Mannering still stood there, leaning against the rail, drenched with water and whipped by the wind. Spar grinned again and looked back to the wild sea.

CHAPTER FOUR

Hurricane Hill

CAPTAIN SPAR had not realized how late it had become. But dawn was nothing more than a graying of the sky and water, and the twilight of day only gave the storm greater strength.

The *Venture* rolled and bucked and shuddered in the sea, plunging ahead a foot for every fathom up and down. Peg Mannering had wearied and Spar had sent her into his cabin.

Soon the black of former acquaintance came on the bridge, overbearing and disdainful, holding on to the dodger.

"Is the ship all right?" said Chacktar.

Spar stared at the scornful face. "Yes, go back and tell them so."

"Remember, you saw Tom Perry kill those men. Otherwise, convict, back you go."

Spar stepped very close to the black. "The title is Captain, if you please."

Chacktar laughed. "Ho, ho, the convict feels his metal."

Spar tried to hold his temper in with but small success. Suddenly, at the sight of the disdainful black face, his control snapped. "Metal, hell! You're going to feel something else!"

He started for Chacktar, but the black dodged nimbly and scurried down the ladder. Spar had no time to calm himself before young Tom Perry, weaving back and forth up the lunging ladder, approached the bridge.

Tom Perry, very drunk but wholly in possession of his strength, grabbed hold of Spar's slicker. "See here, fellow. See here. You can't do that!"

"Can't do what?"

"Can't stay out here. We'll all drown. You've got to make land, hear me? I order you to make land right away. Any old land. Hear me?"

"I'm proceeding to New York, under your father's orders."

"No, no, to hell with my father. He don't care what happens to me. No, he don't care about nothing. He thinks in dollar marks, he does. Listen here, you captain, you make land right away."

"Sorry," said Spar, firmly.

"What's this? What's this? You disobey my orders? Say, I'll have you fired for this. Fired right away."

Spar pried the fingers off his slicker and pushed Tom back against the rail. "Get as drunk as you want, but let me take care of this ship."

"Oh, so it's insubordination, huh? You're gonna get tough, huh? Chacktar! Chacktar! Come up here!"

Chacktar appeared at the head of the ladder. Behind him, Spar could see Folston and Peg Mannering. The three came up to the deck.

Chacktar said, "What do you try to do, Captain? Kill us?"

A fourth person, Felice Bereau, came up and approached Spar with an unsteady walk, holding fast to the rail. "Oh,

Captain, can't you do something about this? We'll all drown!"
She fixed a ravishing glance upon Spar and moved a little
closer, intimately. "You wouldn't want poor Felice to drown,
would you?"

"What makes you think we'll drown?" Spar asked them.

They all looked at Folston who colored a little. Perry said,
"He knows more about the sea than you do, Captain. He says
we're rolling too much. He says we'll go under if we don't
make for Hurricane Hill."

"I believe we're in that vicinity," said Folston.

"Is there any real danger?" said Peg Mannering.

Spar looked them over. "A brave lot you are. A brave lot.
Yes, we're near Hurricane Hill, but if you think I'm a big
enough fool to put in there, you're all mad."

"But what's wrong with it?" asked Peg Mannering.

"*Wrong* with it?" shouted Spar. "Everything is wrong with
it. That's the place all these hurricanes start. There's been
more ships sunk off that island than you can count and more
men drowned."

"Sailor's superstition," mocked Folston.

"Yes, superstition, maybe, but they say when the wind is
blowing you can hear the drowned men screaming for help in
the sea. Superstition, perhaps, but the place has more legends
about it than Greece. There are sailors who tell you that
people live on the place, people who prey on the unfortunate
of the sea. They have found bodies, mangled with knives,
floating off the beach. What do you think of that?"

"Silly," said Folston.

"Come on, you captain, put in there," ordered Perry.

"Couldn't we just go into the lee?" said Felice Bereau. "I believe it's the lee, isn't it, Captain?"

"For God's sake, miss," said Spar, "hang on to the rail if your knees are shaking so you can't stand." And he pried her away from him.

She glared and her nostrils quivered. She went back to stand beside Perry who instantly patted his own chest.

"Lean here, Felice, old kid. I'll protect you."

Chacktar edged away and retreated down the ladder. Spar turned his back on the group and strode into the opposite wing.

"You're fired!" yelled Perry.

Spar paid him no attention whatever and Perry, angry at being ignored, came along the rail, following Spar, one hand in his pocket.

"You're fired!" repeated Perry.

"All right," cried Spar, exasperated, "I'm fired. And you can all go down to hell, for all of me."

Perry aimed an ill-timed swing at Spar's jaw and Spar, acting instinctively, ducked and returned the blow. Perry stumbled back, carried by the abrupt roll of the ship, and slid moaning into the starboard wing. Felice Bereau was instantly beside him, bending over him, glaring at Spar like a cornered leopard.

Peg Mannering stepped back, avoiding Perry. Folston smiled.

The *Venture* keeled again, more sharply than before, and

something in the decks and the feel of the ship told Spar that something was wrong.

He went instantly to the tubes and whistled down. He received no response. He blew again. Still no answer.

The black mate came up and Spar said, "Stay here until I come back."

Spar clattered down the ladder and made his way to the engine room hatch. He went through and stared down at the brightly lighted interior, barred and laced with the ladders.

Folston was at his side, curiously looking down.

Two oilers were bending over a crumpled body on the floor plates. Spar went on down and an instant later recognized the engineer.

The man's skull was crushed and his staring eyes were glazed. Spar examined the wound with swift fingers.

"Must have fallen," said Folston, unconcerned.

"Fallen, hell. He's been smashed with a pistol butt. Here, you fellows, what happened?"

The oilers shook their woolly heads. One of them said, "I don't know. All of a sudden the starboard reduction gear went blooey and then we found Mister Scott lying here like this."

"Take him up to his cabin," said Spar. "We'll have to bury him at sea. Are you certain the reduction gear is broken?"

"Yes, sir, we've only got the port engine left, and with this blow . . ."

"Better take my advice," said Folston. "Put into Hurricane Hill and ride this out in the lee."

41

"Your advice?" said Spar. "So that's where the poor fools got it, eh?"

He went back up to the deck. Chacktar was there with a ready question. Spar pushed by and went to the bridge.

Peg Mannering was there, waiting for him.

"The engineer's been murdered," said Spar, tersely. "We've got to put into Hurricane Hill. We can't ride this with only one engine. And God help me, Miss Mannering, I know that place and the reputation it has."

"What do you mean?"

"Nothing," said Spar, not wishing to frighten her. "Nothing."

With a bleak frown he gave the orders to the helm and the yacht went off her course, heading in toward an island where shipwreck was ordinary and where men died without knowing why, and where no survivors were ever found.

But better the chance, than drowning at sea.

And the storm held them heavily back, as though determined not to release them from its grasp.

CHAPTER FIVE

The Castle

THE source of the blow seemed to be directly ahead, and with their one laboring engine and with their one necessarily rudder-corrected prop, they made very little speed.

The *Venture* shipped the waves over her bows and then, rearing up, spilled hundreds of tons of roaring water aft in great tidal waves which swept the decks clean of everything but the planks themselves. The foremast went first in a shower of tangled, drenched rigging which snaked about in vicious circles until the whole was driven over the side.

From the smashed ports of the bridge, from which even the dodger had been ripped away, Spar could not penetrate the curtain of spray and wind more than thirty feet. His face was set in an ugly twist as he thought about the engineer.

Someone, something on this craft was striving for an unknown end he could not fathom. Someone had wanted the party and Tom Perry out of Martinique. Someone craved their destruction at sea.

Who was it?

And Spar wondered if all these things had happened according to a definite plan. First they had meant to kill him and then they had obviously found a use for him. And would he die as soon as his usefulness was over?

If anyone desired Spar's death, the yacht was certainly

heading for the most likely spot in these waters. Hurricane Hill reeked of it.

The helmsman clung obstinately to the brass wheel, his black shoulders bared by the blow, his muscles rippling with the effort of keeping them on their course.

Buffeted by the gale, Spar stood with his back to the bulkhead, tired out after a battle which had lasted all night and half the day. The fever had taken its toll of his once great strength.

From time to time his expression softened into a grin as he considered his own position here. A convict in charge of a murder ship.

But whatever his position might be at the moment, a few hours were to bring him into one of the strangest predicaments, the most unique situation, that Spar had ever heard of or seen. And Spar had seen and done many strange things.

The blow began to lessen in force at five in the afternoon. And in a half-hour, the wind had died to a six strength. The force of the water had also subsided and soon, in the comparatively clear air, Spar could make out the dim darkness of a headland.

They were in the shelter of Hurricane Hill. To Spar it seemed odd to find reprieve in the lee of so avoided a place.

Folston came up on the wrecked bridge, suave and smiling. "Now, Captain, you can make in toward that point. Beyond it you'll find a better anchorage." He paused apologetically. "Sorry to give you advice but I've been studying a chart down below and I see by the headland that we are a little to the south of it."

Spar frowned and then ordered the helm spun to starboard. Folston was right about the anchorage.

Peg Mannering came up a moment later. "Where are we going?"

"Folston tells me," said Spar, "that we have an anchorage at hand. We'll have to lay to until I can fix the reduction gear."

After the shriek of the hurricane, their ears rang in the comparative silence. All except Folston appeared very tired.

"Where's young Perry? And that Bereau girl?" said Spar.

"Tom's drunk," replied Folston. "Very, very drunk. It's better that way."

"What is?"

"I didn't want to see him bothering Peg."

"Thank you so much," said Peg Mannering with not a little sarcasm.

"Oh, 'twas nothing," replied Folston.

Spar headed the craft around the point and they came into quiet water. Dusk was settling over the high black cliffs which bound them in. In sight of such immensity, the *Venture*, to Spar, seemed very small.

Folston looked long at the high summits about them, but no sign of life was evident.

"I would suggest," said Folston, "that we go ashore for the night. The boat's pretty damp, y'know, and I'm the least bit squeamish about the way the hull has held out."

"Ashore?" said Spar. "You mean sleep over there with the . . . on the rocks?"

"With the dead men?" said Folston. "No, sailor, I assure

you that there are no dead men on Hurricane Hill. You see, er . . . I have a hut over there I use for shooting."

"Shooting," snapped Spar. "There's no game down here."

"Oh, yes, goats and small deer and such. I had a hut constructed so that I could get away from it all, you know. It's really quite comfortable."

"I'm staying with the ship," replied Spar, definitely.

Felice Bereau came up in time to hear Folston's statement. "Oh, I'd love it. When can we go?"

"I'd advise you to stay here," said Spar.

"But why?"

Spar looked at her annoyed face and smiled bleakly. "The ship is comfortable enough."

Perry appeared. "What's this? Go ashore? My God, yes."

"I thought you were drunk," said Spar, looking at Folston.

"Sure I was," grinned Perry. "Now, lower us a boat, you captain, and let's go. I command it—instantly."

Peg Mannering looked longingly at the shore. "Perhaps we'd better go."

"Go ahead," snapped Spar, gruffly. "Helmsman, tell the mate to drop the hook and then lower the tender."

They waited for several minutes until the launch was set in the water. And then all but Spar turned to go. Peg Mannering looked appealingly at him. "Aren't you coming with us?"

"No," said Spar.

She hung back from the rest and looked long at him.

"All right," said Spar. "Let me get a razor and some dry clothes. I need a rest."

She seemed very relieved and when Spar joined them some minutes later in the launch, she was talking gaily with Felice Bereau.

"We'll be back shortly," yelled Spar at the mate on deck. "Stand by and see what the engineers can do with that reduction gear."

"Aye, aye, sir," said the black mate.

When they drew in toward the small landing stage which Spar had not known existed there, the group fell silent. There was something about the dismal blackness of the doleful cliffs which struck them into silence, something about the bleak, treeless heights which made them feel that they were in the presence of something greater than themselves.

The musty odor of the seaweed on the small beach mingled with a salt taste of the air. One lone gull wheeled high above, calling out with his mournful voice, as though warning them back away from Hurricane Hill.

Spar tied their launch to the landing stage and began to help the others out of the craft. And then there came to them a sound, a screaming sound which seemed far away across the water.

Peg Mannering gripped Spar's arm. "What was that?"

Spar did not answer. The sound came again, louder, more awful than before, as though some poor devil was dying in exquisite agony.

Folston assayed to be jocular about it. "The wind in the cliffs, that's all. No need to be afraid. I've heard it many times. Your sailor here will try to tell you that it's the scream of men dying in the gray sea, but that's merely superstition. It's true that the sandy strip here has often been littered with the drowned, but—"

"Shut up!" cried Spar at the sight of Peg's blanching face.

Folston smiled and led the way up a narrow ledge which had been hacked into steps, slimy with the sea. The sea gull swooped lower and cried out again. The far-off scream dwindled away.

And through the heavy darkness which settled upon them like a shroud, they heard a human call high up on the cliff.

"My caretaker," explained Folston. "Hello, up there! We have guests!"

The call came down once more and the sea gull vanished into the dark air. Far below they could see the *Venture* swinging gently at her anchor, a sliver of white on the black sea.

Spar helped Peg up the steps and felt her hands shake as the terrible sound came to them again.

"You say . . . it's the dead, the drowned, calling for help?"

"No, no," said Spar, not wishing to frighten her. "Just the wind in the cliffs, that's all. You heard Folston."

"But I don't trust Folston in anything."

"What's that?" said Folston behind them.

"The lady said she thought you an excellent gentleman to provide a hut so thoughtfully," replied Spar.

"I imagine she did," said Folston. "Well, here's the summit. I've always despised that climb."

In the grayness of the night they could see the hill rising high above them even yet, but something intervened, something which could not be seen from the sea.

It was a spreading black bulk which had the skyline of some medieval castle. No lights shined out from it, and it seemed to Spar that nothing but darkness could be embraced in so dismal a structure.

"Capital, isn't it?" said Folston, leading off. "I found it here, just as it is. Some old refugee from the Spanish Inquisition came here and built it. They say he died and that he wanders about but I've never seen him."

"Cheerful, aren't you?" said Spar.

"Oh, not at all. You see, I found his skull in the banquet hall, as no one had ever had courage enough to come up here and bury him. The skull was crushed at the back. God knows what happened to the skeleton."

"Quit it," said Spar.

"Oh, don't you like it? I find it very interesting, myself. But then I forget that most human beings squirm at such things."

The scream came again, drawn out and shivering, but this time Spar knew that it came from the castle, not the sea. He stopped and halted Peg Mannering with him. They stood before a mammoth gate from which the hinges leaned, within thirty feet of the front door.

"Miss Mannering and I are going back to the ship," said Spar. "I don't give a damn what the others do."

"You think so, eh?" said Folston.

"Yes," said Spar and turned to go.

"I wouldn't," said Folston, evenly, his voice queerly hard.

Spar saw a shimmer of steel in the man's hand. He stepped nearer and saw that it was a gun.

"Stand where you are," said Folston, "or perhaps you'll stay where you are a long, long time."

But Spar did not stand. He sidestepped with a swift motion, and Folston deflected the gun in that direction. Spar whipped back and before Folston could shoot, Spar had the man by the throat. The gun went spinning across the paved courtyard and slammed into the steps.

Spar lifted Folston clear of the ground and shook him. "Now what the hell are you trying to do? What's your game?" Spar shook harder when Folston failed to answer.

Peg Mannering cried out. Bare feet slapped across the stones. Men yelled. The courtyard blazed with lights.

Spar whirled to see a horde of men with bare chests and dark faces swirl out of the doors and down the steps. They held guns and machetes, and from their throats sprang a cry which rolled and shivered through the castle like a siren's blast.

Spar dropped Folston and heard the man bellow an order. The attackers deployed, and in one swift rush completely surrounded the group.

Chacktar detached himself from the path behind them and came forward with an ugly grin, holding an automatic in each hand.

"Now, my fine convict," said Chacktar, "don't you wish you were back in French Guiana? Ah, what we'll do to you here!"

"Shut up!" barked Folston. "Tie his arms behind him and light up the castle."

But Spar was not so easily taken. He sprang at Folston,

but the man evaded him neatly. Chacktar, with a bull bellow, came forward waving his guns, trying to shoot.

The crowd closed in. Spar found himself in the center of hammering fists and slashing knives. Men grabbed him from every side, and though he struck out, kicked and tried to get away, they had him pinioned in a few seconds and bound his arms close to his body.

Then at the point of a sharp knife, they made him march up into the great banquet hall which occupied most of the ground floor.

The hall was of Brobdingnagian proportions. Its ceiling was thirty feet high, cut in Gothic arches, dull with cobwebs and grime. It was paved with flat, worn stones on which many huge chairs were placed. The table in the center of the room was fifty feet long and twenty wide. The wrought-iron chandelier hung low and sent men's shadows flickering along the sides, making their heads as big as barrels.

Perry and Felice Bereau stood thunderstruck, staring about them at the tattered tapestries and the moldy leather chairs. Peg Mannering stood very near Spar.

Folston shed his slicker and idly tossed it to one of the unshaven brutes who stood near and then, after looking slowly about him, smiled. "So you like my little hut, eh? Perhaps that is best, because I am certain you will be here for a long, long time. Do not mind my playmates. They aren't apt to be rough unless you are. On good behavior, the castle is yours. Plenty of room for all. And the doors, Chacktar. The doors."

Chacktar bolted the entrance and chained it shut. He locked

it with a brass key weighing several pounds and brought it to Folston.

"Ah, yes, you aren't apt to escape here. All except our good captain may roam at large. And as he is so used to bars, I am certain that he would feel lonesome unless he had only bars to look upon."

The scream they had heard before came up to them again and Folston frowned. "Who is that?"

A big-chested, hairy-faced man came forward. "Ricardo, Excellency. He has been protesting since we applied the hot iron at your order. It seems he does not like it without his eyes." The man grinned.

"An ungodly racket, Enrico. Besides, we have no need of his money now." Folston waved his hand lightly toward the door and Enrico went out.

They heard his footsteps recede in the empty corridor. The scream came louder and then, suddenly, was cut off short. Enrico reappeared a moment later, wiping his knife upon his sash.

"Very good," said Folston. "A poor merchant. Only worth a few thousand at best. No use playing with him. As I was saying, my guests, the castle is yours. Chacktar, show these good people to their rooms."

Chacktar thrust Perry and Felice Bereau before him and disappeared. Peg Mannering still stood beside Spar.

"And you, Miss Mannering," said Folston, "might like the tower room. A very airy place, quite well appointed."

Peg Mannering dashed the platinum hair out of her blue

eyes and glared, chin up, nostrils quivering. "What are you going to do with Captain Spar?"

"Oh, nothing so bad. I might have a use for him again."

"Set him free," demanded Peg.

Folston smiled. "And if I do?"

"I might again look upon you as a decent man."

"Ah," said Folston. "Enrico, cut Spar's rope there. And watch the man well. Handle him gently and do not shoot to kill. It is too quick. I am not overly fond of the captain, but, as I said, I have a use for him, you see."

Folston conducted Peg Mannering up a winding flight of steps. Spar, seeing that no one detained him, followed. They were ascending up the tower Folston had mentioned and came at last to a small door which stood open.

The room was neatly furnished, rather overawed by a monstrous canopied bed. The wind moaned through the arched windows and went sighing down the steps.

Spar said, "What's the idea of this, Folston?"

Folston turned, smiling. "Try nothing, my captain. Behind you stands Enrico, who is not to shoot to kill. We have no doctor here, you see."

Enrico smiled amiably, gun in hand.

"Rather witless, isn't it?" said Spar. "You can't get away with anything like this, you know."

"No? My dear captain, a man who is wise enough can get away with anything in this world."

The door to the room slammed. A bolt grated. Folston whirled and then glared at Spar.

53

Spar grinned. "With *anything,* my dear count!" he said, and went down the steps, humming to himself, Enrico close behind him, gun ready.

Folston knocked on the door, and then, when he received no answer, followed Spar down.

Spar planted himself wearily in a big chair before the mammoth table and surveyed the unholy crew who stood about. There were fifty or more men there, all of them of the worst.

"Nice selection," mused Spar.

And Folston, who possessed the ego in common with his craving of power, smiled. "Aren't they? They'll all kill at a moment's notice. Recognize any of them?"

"Recognize them? Why should I?"

"Some of your old friends of the penal camps, that's all. Deeply grateful for my rescues. Most of them went there for murder and such like. Delightful fellows." He turned to the men. "One of your past brothers," he said, indicating Spar. "He tipped off the police once that twelve of your former friends were stowed upon his ship, and for pay they sent him to the penal camp, back with your friends."

Spar sat forward, his silver gray eyes as luminous as a wolf's, his hands clutching the table and his mouth set in a twisted snarl.

"So," said Spar, "I have the pleasure of meeting my old friend, the Saint."

Folston bowed, mockingly. "Aye, the Saint."

"And someday," said Spar, "I am going to have the extreme

pleasure of tearing out your throat with my bare hands and watching you kick out your life."

"I am overwhelmed," said the Saint. "At your pleasure."

They nodded to each other and Spar sat back, smiling, looking at Folston's throat, and back at his hands.

CHAPTER SIX

Escape

THE doleful clacks of a big clock were loud in the brooding solemnness of the gray hall. Far away the sea muttered and clawed at the black cliffs, a restless grasping sea shifting uneasily under the midnight sky.

The guard at Spar's door grunted wearily, leaning against the panel, staring with vacant eyes into the gray gloom, holding a rifle carelessly before him on the rough stone.

The bearded, wasted face of the guard was creased with a hundred deep lines, each one more evil than the next. For murder, for assault, to the prison camps, and then, after rescue, to the festering sore called Hurricane Hill.

The panel moved an inch, unheard. A white hand slid easily through the crack, sinuous, softly venomous. The fingers advanced slowly. Suddenly the hand blurred. The guard dropped his gun and jerked his fists to his throat, eyes already staring.

Another hand caught the rifle before it fell, propped it against the wall. The body of the guard was laid its length upon the flinty stone.

Spar stepped all the way out of his room and looked up and down the corridor. Only the moaning wind greeted him there in the drafty dimness. He put away the length of bedspring wire with which he had quietly picked the lock.

Feeling his way, with never a backward glance at the dead guard, Spar went along through the shadows, melting into them.

He reached the main room. One bulb burned in the chandelier, casting down a pool of yellow light over the mammoth table, deepening the blackness of the arches, thickening rather than lightening the dense gloom.

Spar saw that the place was empty of men. He approached the staircase with cautious steps and started up. A faint stream of light came from the top landing and with it the scuff of leather on stone.

Spar continued his silent ascent, peering before him with all the intensity of his silver gray eyes. At last he saw that the light came from a slit under the door and that a shadow stood before it. Doubtless, it was a guard.

Without the least sound, Spar reached the landing. The guard suddenly moved forward, sensing another presence. Spar struck out. The sharp crack of the blow echoed through the dismal hallways and then the monotonous clacking of the clock was once more all the sound.

He eased the unconscious guard to the floor. The fellow's mouth was running a thin trickle of sticky blood. The blow had been clean. Using a belt and the rifle sling, Spar securely bound the man.

He was about to rap on Peg Mannering's door when he heard footsteps below. Looking down the stairway he could see that Enrico and Count Folston—the Saint—had entered the great hall. Not daring to make another move, Spar knelt and watched intently.

The words came up to him, hollow in the great emptiness of the place.

"Have you sent it?" said Folston.

"Ten minutes ago," replied Enrico. "Chacktar attended to it. He should be back shortly with the answer."

"If the fools in Martinique relay that radio, yes."

"I do not quite understand. . . ." said Enrico, cautiously.

"What matter if you do not?" flared Folston.

"I . . . was merely thinking. . . ."

"You were not brought here to think," said Folston.

"The men were wondering, that was all."

Folston studied the other, rapping his well-kept nails on the table the while. Then, evidently deciding that the men were entitled to some sort of explanation, he leaned forward. "We are all about to become very rich."

Enrico nodded as though he had fully expected that.

"Frederick Perry thinks a great deal of his son in spite of the fool's actions. He thinks that Tom upholds the precious virtue of the Perry family and that Tom will come around in a few years. Old Perry was very wild in his youth."

"But why is Tom Perry here?" asked Enrico.

"Fool," replied Folston. "If I say that I will turn young Perry over to the French authorities, to save his name old Perry will do almost anything. If I hand young Perry to the French, they will send him to the penal colony. Is not that enough?"

"But what has he done?"

Spar, who only saw that these two were blocking his one avenue of escape, writhed with impatience. But now he began to listen intently.

The Saint went on. "Tom Perry thinks he killed two men in Martinique. As a matter of fact, he did not. We were visited by this fellow who calls himself Captain Spar. Henri received a letter from DeJong in Paramaribo, saying that this fellow I had caused to be put away was heading north, intent on killing me.

"At the moment I had need of a corpse. And so I had Henri send this Captain Spar to a certain tavern with a package full of nothing. Spar was to wait there for other men, but in reality, Spar was waiting for his own execution.

"Henri and one of his dear friends set out to kill Spar, thus giving me the corpse I wanted, but, unfortunately, Spar killed them."

"Henri dead?" cried Enrico.

"Yes, yes, very sad. But he was getting temperamental. Wanted more money anyway. He would have sold us if the price had been to his liking. But as I say, Spar killed the pair.

"Then we drugged young Perry and our very efficient Chacktar had the boy carried to the tavern and brought to. It thus appeared, even to Tom, that he had murdered a couple men. He was very pathetic about it, too, and then became very defiant. But he believed he had done it, nonetheless.

"And, too, we had a witness in Spar, who had really done the killing. Spar had nothing to lose and so he said that young Perry had done the deed. As I did not think I had any further use of Spar, I intended to have him killed that night. But Larson, the fool, stalked out of the place and said that he would have nothing more to do with Perry.

"I had already seen to it that the *Venture*'s mate was in the hospital because that mate is a hardheaded fool, and Larson's walkout left me without anyone to captain the *Venture*. And you'll agree, Enrico, my old, that the *Venture* is very necessary to us, eh? Be careful of Spar. Do not kill him all the way. Leave him enough body and brains to navigate the *Venture*.

"What do you think of the Saint now, Enrico?"

"Marvelous!" cried Enrico, the perfect yes-man. "But about Perry."

"To save his name and his son, he will deed over half of the Perry Sugar Central to me. And here, my old, is where the *Venture* comes in so neatly. When the deed is made, if anything should happen to Frederick Perry—some unfortunate accident, you see—and if anything should happen to Tom Perry, then the Perry Sugar Central and the bank account of a half million is all mine."

"And what happens to us?" demanded Enrico.

"You? Why, you will help me, of course."

"On French territory? Liable to momentary arrest?"

The Saint smiled indulgently. "Of course. Why, I would see to it that you went wherever you wanted to go. That you would all have plenty of money. Or, if you wanted to stay here, I would see to it that the castle would be stocked well with pleasant things."

"Good," said Enrico. "Good!"

"We sail with the *Venture* in a short while, land at Fort-de-France at night, make our way to the Perry house, surround it, make certain the deed is made out and waiting, and then we go away, leaving Perry mysteriously dead—at the hands of Captain Spar. We will all be far away by then. We will get another captain in Martinique—any black schooner captain could do it for us. We return here, wait for some little while, and then I go back to claim my part of the bargain. Then I return here with whatever we need."

"Excellent," said Enrico. "Is there anything you wish me to do?"

"Why, yes, you might make very certain that Captain Spar sleeps well. We need him worse than we need Perry."

Spar instantly remembered the dead guard in front of his open door. He felt his palms moisten. Reaching for the rifle at his side, he snicked the bolt and held the weapon across his chest.

He could easily shoot the Saint, but he suddenly remembered that he was no longer responsible only for himself. He had other lives in his care. To turn this mad horde of penal colony convicts loose with the rest of the party still imprisoned would be a terrible thing.

His own fate was secondary to him. He considered himself as good as dead already. What would it avail him to get free from this place? All he knew was the sea, and when he returned to New York, he would be very apt to discover his record had preceded him. France would probably extradite him for his escape.

But no, he told himself, gripping that wet rifle stock there in the dark. These were not the real reasons. He was trying to persuade himself that he no longer dreamed. There, on the other side of that door, was Peg Mannering. He was watching the Saint and he told himself that five years of plotting should certainly find him true to a blood vow. But he did not hate the Saint for the things the Saint had done to Captain Spar. He hated the man for what he might do to Peg Mannering.

Perplexed, shaken by the blinding truth of it, Spar listened to the footsteps of Enrico, going up the corridor toward a dead guard who, in his stiff silence, would shout betrayal and the news of escape.

Spar's heart was banging against his ribs until he thought Count Folston himself must hear it.

The footsteps of Enrico were receding. Spar listened for the shout which must follow. He watched the Saint, watched the confident expression of the thin face, watched the nervousness of the long, well-kept hands. Odd that so much deviltry could hide behind so bored a mask.

Spar was thinking about Peg Mannering. That night in Martinique when she had worn a blue dinner gown and a string of pearls. He remembered how her platinum hair had shimmered in the light, how her frank, deep eyes had regarded him with a queer intensity.

In a moment now, Enrico would shout and Spar's fine plans for escape would crumple into a choking dust heap.

Spar thought about Tom Perry. About the whining, blustering drunkard who would someday possess Peg Mannering as his wife. Even if they got out of this, that would happen.

Spar felt all alone, defeated, fighting against a whole world and himself.

Enrico's piercing cry ripped through the solemn gray tomb like a diamond drill rips through sandstone.

CHAPTER SEVEN

Trapped

THE Saint was on his feet, his chair falling away from him. Men were shouting to one another through the castle. Enrico's calls were urgent but unintelligible.

The Saint whipped a Colt .45 out of his jacket and sprinted after Enrico. Men came tumbling through the great hall, calling to one another, the light glancing from their bare backs.

A cyclone had been started with Spar's room as its vortex. Everyone followed the Saint, yelling, looking to their weapons. They reminded Spar of sharks whisking off to devour a bloody prey.

The sharks might go, but the wolf was still there. In an instant the great hall was empty. The Saint's voice was heard above all others. Spar wasted no time whatever.

Leaping down the steps, Spar rushed across the rough stone, his hammering feet lost in the discord of others' making. He gripped the chains and bars of the big door, hurled them down. He slammed the entrance open and was fanned by a breath of moist air. For an instant he stared across the courtyard, down the path toward the beach. It would be so easy to go, to get away from the Saint.

But that was what they expected him to do. Spar turned back and vaulted up the steps three at a time until he was again at Peg Mannering's door. He hammered on it with the rifle butt.

"It's Spar! Open up for God's sake!"

Because of the bedlam on the lower floor he could hear no movement in the room. He stood drowned in his own apprehensive sweat, expecting momentary discovery.

They were coming back now, back toward the great hall. And they came running, with the Saint in the lead. Spar looked at the impassive, double-barred panel which stood between him and momentary safety. This was the first place they'd come. And he could not live long enough to get Peg Mannering out if they found him against that door.

Why hadn't he killed the Saint when he had the chance? It was too late now.

He heard the creak of a rusty hinge. A white face appeared in the crack. He pushed hurriedly through and slammed and bolted the door behind him.

Peg Mannering stood with her back against the wall, staring at him. To one who had been reared far from the sight and thought of violence, Spar presented a terrifying picture. His hair was rumpled, hanging in his eyes. His knuckles dripped blood. His shirt was torn open at the throat. And his silver gray eyes held the luminous light of the killer.

"Keep quiet," ordered Spar. "They are looking for me. Do not open up for them on any pretext."

He tucked the rifle under his arm and went to the window. Peg Mannering moved like a sleepwalker. She blew out the candle and then went back to the wall. The only light was that of the dark sky. Spar stood in the arched window, looking down upon the courtyard.

Hammering at the door made him start. Folston's voice cried, "Spar! If you're in there, come out! Peg! Open up before he kills you! He's gone mad! He doesn't understand this joke of mine. It's only a joke, Peg. Open up!"

"He isn't here," said Peg Mannering in a firm voice.

The hammering stopped. Silence reigned for a moment. Then the door creaked under the pressure of strong shoulders. But the builder of that castle had thought of such things and the door was constructed of flinty ironwood.

After some moments, the pressure ceased and footsteps were heard going down the stairs. Then Spar, looking from the window, saw men dash across the courtyard in full cry, waving torches over their unkempt heads.

The Saint paused for an instant and shouted: "Fan out to the right and left. Find him! He's somewhere about. He won't make the *Venture* because of the guard on the cliffs."

"So there's a guard on the cliff," muttered Spar. "Thank you, Saint, perhaps I'll strangle you after all."

The quiet intensity of his voice made Peg wince. But she moved closer to him, rested her hand on his shoulder, and looked down at the torches that danced like fireflies over the island.

"What happened?" said Peg.

"I killed my guard and they found the body before I could rescue you."

"You killed a man?"

"You don't call these beasts men, do you? Wait a bit. Maybe we can get out." And then it was Spar's turn to wince. Propped against the wall, tied with a sling and belt, Peg Mannering's guard was certain to be discovered before the night was out. That would direct them straight to her door. Nothing would stop them. In their haste they had overlooked him once. They wouldn't make the same mistake on closer inspection.

"We've got to get to the *Venture*," said Spar. "They'll know I'm here."

"But can't we take the others with us?"

"The others? I'm not interested in the others. I'll send the navy back for them." Spar looked at her with a frankness born of danger.

She backed away from him. "But you must!"

"You and I have a chance to get out. We can't get out with Felice Bereau and that drunkard to give us away. They aren't worth it."

With a certain hauteur, she said, "You forget that I am engaged to marry Tom."

"You had almost forgotten it. Forget it again. I've known from the moment I set eyes on you that someday I would tell you that I love you. I'm telling you now. I can get the two of us out, but not four. You are the one I take. Let Tom Perry rot."

Stiffly, she replied, "I have given my word that I would marry him. I do not go back on my word. Do you take me for some street gamine?"

"I take you for a woman who will not listen to her own heart. You pretend that you are afraid of me, that you think me beneath you. Perhaps I am. But don't forget that the Saint is watching you. Don't forget that you are not choosing between Tom Perry and Captain Spar. You are choosing between Captain Spar and the Saint."

"Count Folston . . . the Saint?"

"Yes, the Saint. You've heard of him, I see. If your choice is not correct, you'll hear more of him, much more."

"You take a great deal for granted, Captain Spar," she replied. "Such vanity should be rewarded. And are you implying that you are so lacking in gallantry that you require me to buy my freedom with my hand?"

Spar looked at her uncertainly for a moment and then abruptly laughed. "We are both being very noble. You are taking the side of a worthless, drunken wretch and I am taking the part of a half-mad convict. Perhaps it would be better if we were to consider the best for everyone concerned. I can get out of here with you only. Four cannot move as quickly or as silently as two. We must do something. And the best we can do is to get aboard the *Venture* and sail for Martinique, to bring the French authorities here."

"But wouldn't they . . . ?"

"Yes, they'd send me back. But you are thinking of your promise, and, strangely, so am I. I can do nothing. I might as well do the only decent thing. I killed those two men in Martinique, not Tom."

"You?"

"Yes, Folston pinned it on Tom to get him here. It was all planned. I was to be the corpse, but I let two killers substitute for me. I'll see to it that everything goes off like clockwork. All shipshape. Come on, we haven't much time."

He started to the door, but she snatched at his arm and held him back. "No, no. That is not a good plan. Can't we hide on the island for a time, let Folston do what he wants, and get away by stealing some small boat? You can't give yourself up!"

Spar faced her, looked into her eyes and saw there the expression ladies reserve for the man they love. Suddenly he swept her into his arms and kissed her. She offered no resistance for a moment, and then she pushed him away.

"No," she said, "I'm the one who is half-mad. We must get Tom out of here, no matter what it costs. I have given my promise."

Spar unbarred the door. The stairway was empty and so, apparently, was the great hall beyond. Closely followed by Peg, he went slowly down, listening at each step.

A shot rapped outside, swallowed instantly by a chorus of yells and another report.

"They're shooting at shadows," whispered Spar. "They've forgotten they need a captain."

He went halfway across the great hall before he saw the guard at the door. The ex-convict, naked to the waist and gripping a rifle barrel, was staring out at the courtyard as though anxious to be in on the excitement and perhaps have the pleasure of killing Spar.

Spar held Peg back, mutely pointing. Then, cat-footed, he went forward, rifle ready. Some sixth sense, possessed by jungle cats and criminals alike, must have warned the sentry of his danger. When Spar was still ten feet from him, the man whirled about, open-mouthed in his surprise. Then in the same second he dropped into a crouch and swiftly whipped up his weapon. A shark was facing the wolf.

Spar held Peg back, mutely pointing. Then, cat-footed,
he went forward, rifle ready.

Spar had also stopped, realizing the bridge was too wide to traverse in the instant still remaining to him. His rifle butt dropped in a blur, described a half circle and, speeding forward like a javelin, streaked toward the sentry's chest.

The man tried to dodge, but he was blinded by the light he faced and paralyzed by the suddenness of the move. The steel-shod butt caught him in the ribs and he dropped with a hoarse groan.

Spar turned and took Peg by the hand. He led her over the inert body, stooped and retrieved his rifle, and then went on into the courtyard.

Another shot beat through the roar of the surf and the shouts. Spar instinctively ducked and then stood up when he realized that a shadow had been the target.

"I'd rather be the quarry than a searcher," muttered Spar. "They're like the gingham dog and the calico cat. They'll eat each other up."

Peg, small in his big shadow, looked inquiringly at him, mystified by a man who could kill and quote child's poetry in the same breath. She began to realize that man is, at best, a predatory beast and that, in civilization as in the Ice Age, killing is sometimes necessary. She saw things clearly, without any distortion, for the first time in her life. And seeing life so cheaply bought, she responded with an atavistic disregard for anything which might interfere with their safety.

Spar flanked the trail, going through the thin brush. Once he stopped and crept ahead. When he returned to her and led her forward, she saw a smoking torch, fallen from an outstretched, slowly contracting hand. She did not wince.

With shouts on every side of them, with lights bobbing all about them, they came to the top of the cliff trail. Once more, Spar left her to crouch in the shelter of a rock.

He groped forward, feeling for the guard he knew to be there. Inch by inch, stone by stone, he made his way down the trail, striving to pierce the gloom.

Ahead he heard a sharp tinkle of metal against metal. A man had moved somewhere close to him. Spar went more slowly than before, hands describing a slow arc all about him.

Suddenly he touched cloth. In the same instant the guard jerked down with the rifle butt and caught Spar across the face. The rifle rose for a second blow, but Spar went in under it and reached for the throat.

Caught in each other's sinewy embrace, they rocked on the edge, each one trying to throw the other to one side. The guard was strong, almost too strong. Spar closed in, tighter, more relentlessly.

The guard screamed for help. Screamed again. Spar picked him bodily from the cliff face and dropped him into space. The scream went on for a long, long time, growing less and less. Then the greedy sucking of the surf in the rocks gobbled the sound.

Shouts came in a medley from above. Spar was certain that Peg would be caught before he could get back to her. But an instant later he felt a cool hand groping for his own and they started down, recklessly, sliding over loose stone, scrambling along a steep trail they could not see.

Men were coming down from above. Debris slithered over the edge and dropped about the two. Torches lined the top like a string of electric lights at a carnival.

Spar and Peg came to the landing stage. Spar dropped the girl into the boat and slid behind the wheel. He started the engine and slipped the gears into reverse. They went rocketing out into the swell, pitching. He turned and sent the launch bucking toward the lights of the *Venture*.

Rifle shots pounded behind them, sending long streamers of phosphorescence through the depths of the harbor. Spar was grinning. "Presently, presently," he said. "They have no other boat."

They curved in alongside the gangway and, tossing the painter to a dark figure on the deck, Spar helped the girl up the ladder ahead of him.

Puffing, feeling very satisfied with himself, he reached the deck. "Well, we're safe," he said.

But Peg did not seem to hear him. She stopped at the top, rigid with surprise.

Spar walked straight into an unwavering rifle muzzle, and saw other rifles ready and waiting, beyond.

Chacktar's smiling mask was thrust toward them. Chacktar stepped out of his crowd of men and bowed, mockingly, borrowing his manner from the Saint.

"Welcome aboard, Captain," said Chacktar. "Welcome aboard, Miss Mannering. Would you like to go to your cabins immediately, or shall I have tea served upon the sun deck?"

Spar drooped, his bloodied face sagging into weariness.

"Pierre!" said Chacktar. "Take the launch back to the Saint.

Tell him I have received a return radio from Perry stating that the deed is made out, only waiting for Count Folston's signature. He will doubtless wish to sail instantly."

Peg Mannering, unsteadily stepping to one side, clutched at Spar's sleeve. Very quietly, she fainted.

Spar took her up and carried her to the bridge, conscious of Chacktar's knowing leer, conscious of a dozen unwavering muzzles, conscious of extreme defeat.

CHAPTER EIGHT

Branded with Murder

IT was night. The sullen black bulk of Martinique rose up on the port bow of the anchored *Venture*. A few lights glittered in the fishing village just north of Fort-de-France, and sent their long streamers like silver swords into the gentle surf.

The group on the darkened bridge were silent. They stood apart from one another, waiting patiently, oppressed by the presence of armed men. Felice Bereau whimpered softly to herself. Peg Mannering kept her eyes on Spar's back. Tom Perry muttered obscene phrases helplessly, knowing that he was fated for ill, in spite of the fact that he was drunk.

The Saint came up to them and pointed at the launches in the water. "The ladies had better stay here. Never fear that I will be back. Spar and Perry are coming with me."

Spar's voice was metallic, toneless. "I would suggest that you take the ladies with you. You cannot trust these men."

Folston shrugged. "Perhaps that is true. That is very well. Come along, good people. I have a party planned."

They went down into the boats in a silent file and were presently ashore, standing on the deserted sand. Armed men stood silently about, watchful, waiting for orders.

Spar nervously glanced back at the *Venture* from time to time and licked his dry lips.

They went by jungle trail up through the steep hills, making their way to the Perry plantation without entering Fort-de-France. Spar, as minute followed minute, hoped that customs men would see them and stop them. Even though that meant his own recapture, it was preferable to the role he knew he would be forced to play.

They came in the darkness to the house, and the men scouted the place with great caution. The Saint was seeking to locate Perry and murder him before the servants could scatter out and warn the police. In fact, he hoped that the killing would be so silent that the servants would not at all be aware of it.

Presently his scouts came back with doleful tidings. This was Saturday night. The one night the Saint should not have picked. And all his plans seemed doomed to fall because of that unwitting choice.

"Saturday night," rasped the Saint. "They're at the Bal Ludu! And Perry? Where is Perry?"

"That I do not know," said Chacktar.

The Saint thought for several minutes and then, with a brightening manner, said, "Very well, it is better that way. Chacktar, your staying here would excite no suspicion. Very well, we enter the place."

They went into the glittering living room and from there into Perry's office. The Saint, drawing on a pair of rubber gloves in case the police should look for fingerprints, began to rip files from their racks, papers from the drawers, until he had made a fine clutter on the floor. Then he knelt before the safe and proceeded to open it, referring from time to time to a paper he held, using the numbers he had often watched Perry use.

In the safe he found the made-out partnership deed. He found another paper giving details which were unpleasant to him. This he destroyed. He pocketed the deed to half the moneymaking plantation and then rose up with a smile.

"Chacktar, place young Perry and Captain Spar in a good, solid room. It is close to midnight now. Perry will soon be home. Chacktar, when Frederick Perry enters the house, slit his throat, toss down the knife and fade away. We will go back to the *Venture*."

At that last remark, a faint smile twitched Spar's lips. But he was hurried away with Tom to a bedroom. The shutters were barred, the door was locked upon them, and they were left alone.

"Remember, I shall be watching for you," said Chacktar from the garden.

They heard the Saint say, "Come, ladies, we go a-sailing once more."

An instant later they heard the sound of an engine coming up the hill. Perry was returning!

The Saint's clear tones were heard again, as though he spoke into a telephone. "Police?" he said in patois. "*M'sieu* Perry is dead! Yes, yes! Dead! Come instantly!" The phone clicked.

Footsteps sounded and then, except for the roar of the approaching engine, all was silence.

Perry sank down upon the bed, moaning, "They'll get me now! They'll get me! They'll think I killed my father. They'll put me in jail for killing those men. They'll hang me! And nobody will believe a word I say."

Spar was suffering the same thoughts, but he did not voice them. Added to his misery was the fact that Peg Mannering would be lost to him forever. Folston was faultless in his plotting. The police would come, recognize two men they already knew to be criminals, and refuse to believe a word told them.

A corpse, two men, an opened safe, and the conclusions would be perfectly drawn. And Folston would present his deed in due course, claim the other half by partnership laws, and reign supreme.

It was all so neat, so flawless. The car was stopping. The police were already on their way. But nothing could be worse, thought Spar. Even his own death.

He aimed a solid kick at the shutter. It shivered and remained intact.

"Why do that?" moaned Tom Perry. "Folston will be gone in the *Venture* before anyone could stop him. Even if . . ."

Yellow so-and-so, thought Spar. Not even worried about his own father's imminent death.

The shutter caved suddenly. Spar leaped through and hit the ground on his hands and knees. He scrambled up.

He saw Chacktar standing in the headlights, automatic raised, aiming at the occupant of the machine. Spar sprinted forward, yelling as he went.

Chacktar twisted about, undecided, two tasks suddenly confronting him. Spar raced in under the gun just as it fired. The flaming powder scorched his cheek. He struck solidly and sent Chacktar reeling back.

Spar aimed a second blow and missed. Chacktar hammered down with the automatic barrel, kicking and squirming to get away. His eyes flashed white.

Then Spar's hands went in through the guard. Spar's fingers closed on Chacktar's windpipe. Chacktar threshed helplessly in the grip.

Little by little, his life ebbed out. Spar dropped him with a feeling of disgust.

Other cars were coming. It was all up, thought Spar. But perhaps it had been worth it, even though he went back to the prison camps. The penal colony could hold no terrors now.

Frederick Perry ran forward, crying, "What's this? What's this?"

Spar faced him. "Your son is in that house. You'd better get him out. The police are coming."

"My son? But I thought—"

"Don't think, act!" rapped Spar impatiently.

But it was already too late. Cars drew up and belched forth men. The gendarmes clustered about the two, throwing out a barrage of questions.

"There is no corpse," said Spar.

"No corpse?" cried the chief. "Name of a cat! Is all this some joke, *hein*?"

Gendarmes had gone into the house and were now calling

for the chief. Taking the two with him, the chief entered. Young Perry was standing in the center of the living room, shaking with terror.

The gendarmes recognized him instantly with glad shouts, but Spar's voice broke through the babble.

"Listen," said Spar, "the yacht *Venture*, if I am not mistaken, has just sunk three miles north of Fort-de-France. A great criminal and many armed men are there on the beach. I would advise that you telephone the colonial barracks and have the people rounded up. It is of the utmost importance."

"What's this?" cried the chief. "What's this? How do you know?"

"Because, on my last trip into the engine room, I opened two seacocks. The *Venture* has been filling up for hours and she must have gone down by this time. The men left aboard have not intelligence enough to shut them off."

"Wait!" said the chief, pulling his black mustache, "I know you. I have lately received your description from French Guiana. You are Captain Spar. Aha, my fine jailbird, so you think to so escape us."

"Yes," cried Spar. "I'm an escaped convict, but down there on the beach you will find two score escaped convicts. Get them, phone the barracks, or you'll lose your precious badge!"

The man blinked at Spar, recognized the sincerity of tone, and reached for the instrument. He barked his information, and ten minutes later, a battalion of French colonials were racing down from the hills to the beach.

Twenty minutes later, the wondering inhabitants of the fishing village were startled by the sound of rifle fire.

An hour later, a major and many soldiers marched up the road to the Perry plantation, escorting what prisoners they had left.

The Saint, flanked by the mustard uniforms of the colonials, was very disheveled. His debonair manner had given place to a definitely terrified mien. His eyes were very large when he saw Spar and Frederick Perry on such excellent terms.

Then some of the bravado came back and he shook loose confining hands. "So the convict thinks himself smarter than the Saint, eh? Turns state's evidence and gets the reprieve. Someday, Captain Spar, you and I may be able to settle this matter by ourselves."

"Why not now?" said Spar, getting up slowly.

"No, no," cried the chief. "You are my prisoner. Do not damage yourself!"

But the colonial major was of a more warlike mind. "Let them go ahead. Perhaps we shall learn something."

But he might have saved his words. Unmindful of the men all about them, Folston and Spar hurled themselves from the two sides of the room and met in the center of the polished floor like two charging cavalry brigades.

The Saint was lighter than Spar, but the Saint had the advantage of tricks which Spar would never have used. They rained blows on one another in a matter of seconds. Too surprised to interfere, the soldiers and police stood still.

Spar was striking for one spot, the heart. His blows were steady. The wolf, taking his one hold. The shark rapped every place at once, using fair means and foul.

Suddenly, Spar sank his fist to the knuckles in the Saint's

coat. Folston, unnerved by the blow, slipped back to the floor. Spar threw himself on top of the man, hands seeking out the throat. And the shark screamed for mercy.

Men darted forward to pry them apart, but Spar was shouting, "Stay back! Stay back and listen! Now, Saint Folston, tell them you framed me. Tell them I didn't know about that cargo in Paramaribo!"

In choked words, feeling his death near at hand, the Saint talked. He talked for fifteen minutes and each time he tried to stop, Spar's thumbs went deeper into his throat. And then when the police and the soldiers had the story, and not until then did Spar stand up.

Peg Mannering was instantly at his side. Spar, in terse phrases, told his own side of the events, ending up with, "I know you are neither judges nor juries, but what you have heard tonight is true, and after hearing it I am confident that men of your intelligence and understanding will certainly see to it that France does not unjustly condemn me, that France will free me of my sentence."

The major shouted, "France will not desert you!" in a fervor of patriotism which he so seldom found a chance to indulge.

"Nor will the police!" cried the chief. "I take the responsibility of setting you free this minute. You and this so young Tom Perry."

"Thank you," said Spar, with a smile.

But Peg Mannering was not smiling. Peg Mannering knew that everything rested as it had before for her. This had changed nothing.

"But where is Tom?" said Frederick Perry.

"Probably in the office," said the chief of police. "I saw him there but a moment ago."

Frederick Perry disappeared and returned carrying an empty cash box, eyes wide with questioning.

The guard at the door came in and said, "Was it all right to let those people through?"

"What people?" demanded the police chief.

"The young man and the dark-haired girl. They said they had to make a boat and I saw that they were not being held."

"A boat!" cried Frederick Perry. "The liner which sails at dawn. That Bereau woman has . . . has . . . kidnaped him."

"Ah," said the chief of police, "I shall bring them back."

But Frederick Perry shook his head. "No. No, do not bring them back. Let them go. He has taken all the money he will ever get from me. He has caused me all the trouble he ever will. Let him go."

Peg Mannering, face radiant, stood very close to Spar. The major and his prisoners departed with military precision. The police, taking Chacktar's corpse with them, roared away.

"And now where?" said Spar, not really caring.

Frederick Perry stopped in the center of the floor and looked fixedly at Spar. "Where? Why, young man, nowhere. I want you to stay here. You have done me a greater service than you know.

"For years I have looked forward to the time when I could leave this island and this work. For years I thought Tom would finally come to his senses and look elsewhere than into his cups, but I realize now that I was nursing a dream. I've been hard, perhaps I am being unjust in letting him go away with that woman. But perhaps he loves her. Perhaps she will do things for him I never could do.

"But that does not solve my problems. I must get away from this place. And, after the things you have done, after saving me—what you did, I can but ask you another favor."

Spar, startled, looked up from Peg's face and said, "Another favor?"

"Yes, live here in this house, manage my interests, consider yourself as my son. Will you?"

"After certain legal ties are tied, yes."

"Oh, it would all be legal. I will see to it that—"

"No, no," said Peg Mannering, laughing. "He means . . . or I think he means . . . hope he means . . ."

Frederick Perry's face relaxed into a benign smile.

Story Preview

Story Preview

NOW that you've just ventured through one of the captivating tales in the Stories from the Golden Age collection by L. Ron Hubbard, turn the page and enjoy a preview of *Hell's Legionnaire*. Join Dusty Colton, an American who flees the French Foreign Legion to escape a harsh prison sentence only to rush headlong into a Berber tribal lair. Despite his long odds of solo escape, he can't leave a captive American woman behind and must find a way for both of them to outrun the Berber tribe and the Foreign Legion.

Hell's Legionnaire

B EHIND them, the ambush was sprung with the speed of a steel bear trap. One moment the Moroccan sunlight was warm and peaceful upon this high pass of the Atlas Mountains. The next lashed the world with the sound of flaming Sniders and Mannlichers and flintlocks.

Gray and brown djellabas swirled behind protecting rocks. Bloodshot eyes stared down sights. Scorching lead reached in with hammers and battered out lives with the gruesome regularity of a ticking clock.

Ann Halliday's shrill scream of terror was lost in an ocean of erupting sound. Her terrified Moorish barb plunged under her, striving to dash through the jamming corridor of the peaks.

Horses fell, maimed and screaming. Men died before they could reach their holsters, much less their guns. The two auto-rifles in the vanguard had been jerked from their packs but now they were covered with dust and blood and their gunners stared with glazed, dead eyes at the enemy, the Berbers.

John Halliday, Ann's father, tried to ride back to her. Within five feet of her pony, he stiffened in his saddle, shot through the back. The next instant his face was torn away by a ricocheting slug. He pitched off at her feet.

Muskets and rifles rolled like kettledrums. Black powder

smoke drifted heavily above the pass, a shroud to temporarily mark the passing of twenty men.

A voice was bellowing orders in Shilha and, dying a shot at a time, the volleying finally ceased. Then there was only dust and smoke and the blood-drenched floor of the pass.

Two Berbers, blue eyes hard and metallic in the hoods of their djellabas, jerked Ann Halliday from her barb. She struggled, but their sinews were trained by lifetimes spent on the Atlas and she might as well have tried to break steel chains.

Her boots made swirls of dust as she attempted to impede their progress. Once she looked back and saw a Berber delivering the death stroke to a wounded expedition aide. She did not look back again.

The Berbers half lifted, half threw her to the saddle of a waiting horse. Other mountain men were coming up, their arms filled with plunder. As though in a nightmare, Ann saw them mount their ponies.

They filed down the pass, up a slope, and trotted toward a mountain peak which loomed brown and sullen before them. The rapidity of the events was too much for her. They dazed her and made her slightly ill. But she had not yet realized that her party had been slain, that she was in the hands of revolting tribesmen. Mercifully, a sort of anesthetic had her in its grip.

Almost before she realized they were on their way, they stopped. Teeth flashed in laughter. Men were patting rifles and ammunition and bulky sacks of loot. Some of them pointed to her and laughed more loudly. She did not understand, not yet.

She did not struggle when they led her to the square block of a house. She thought that within she might have time to rest and collect herself, that she might be able to devise some means of escape. But when the cool interior surrounded her, she stared across the room and knew that her experience had not yet begun.

A Berber was sitting there, knees drawn up, djellaba hood thrown back. His eyes were gray and ugly. His cheeks were thin and his strong arms were bundles of muscle as he extended them before him. He was white, true, and his hair and beard were brown. But from him there exuded a web of evil, almost tangible in its strength.

"Get thee from me!" snapped the crouching one to her two guards. They went without a backward glance, doubtless glad to be free and able to take their part in the loot division.

The bearded one on the mat looked appraisingly at Ann. He saw her delicate face, her full lips, her dark blue eyes. His study swept down. She was clothed in a cool, thin dress which clung tightly to her beautifully molded body.

Her breasts were firm and tight against the cloth. The material clung to her thighs, outlining smooth, mysteriously stirring indentations and curves.

The Berber licked thin lips, scarcely visible through the thickness of his beard. His eyes came back with a jerk to her face.

"I," he said slowly, "am Abd el Malek, the man who shall soon sweep the *Franzawi* from the plains and mountains of Morocco." His French was flawless. "I wonder that they did not kill you, but now . . ." He let his metallic eyes linger on her thighs. "Now I am overjoyed that they did not."

She threw back her head, her eyes alight with anger: "Abd el Malek, dubbed 'The Killer.' It might please you to know that I am not a *Franzawi*. I am an American and if anything should happen to me . . . I suppose you think you can wipe out an expedition and fail to have *la Légion* after you."

"*La Légion!*" He spat as though the name tasted bad. "What do I care about *la Légion*? There is no company within five days' march. Resign yourself, my little one, to the time you pass with me."

Her eyes lost a little of their rage. Something of terror began to creep into them. "But . . . but there might be . . . ransom."

"Ha! Ransom! What do I care for ransom? In my stronghold over the Atlas I have the price to buy every man, woman and child in Morocco. No, sweet morsel, I am not interested in ransom. Ordinarily I would not be interested in you, Christian dog that you are. I would not touch you."

He stood up, towering over her. She backed up against the mud wall.

"No," he said, "I would not be interested. But this campaign has been long, rather boring. My women are far away, and . . ." He smiled, fastening his hot eyes on her body.

Reaching out he tried to hold her wrist. She jerked it away and aimed a slap at his leathery cheek. He laughed, displaying discolored, uneven teeth. "So," he said, "you will have it another way."

To find out more about *Hell's Legionnaire* and how you can obtain your copy, go to www.goldenagestories.com.

Glossary

Glossary

STORIES FROM THE GOLDEN AGE *reflect the words and expressions used in the 1930s and 1940s, adding unique flavor and authenticity to the tales. While a character's speech may often reflect regional origins, it also can convey attitudes common in the day. So that readers can better grasp such cultural and historical terms, uncommon words or expressions of the era, the following glossary has been provided.*

Atlas Mountains: a mountain range in northwest Africa extending about fifteen hundred miles through Morocco, Algeria and Tunisia including The Rock of Gibraltar. The Atlas ranges separate the Mediterranean and Atlantic coastlines from the Sahara Desert.

Barbary Coast: the term used by Europeans, from the sixteenth until the nineteenth century, to refer to the coastal regions in North Africa that are now Morocco, Algeria, Tunisia and Libya. The name is derived from the Berber people of North Africa. In the West, the name commonly refers to the pirates and slave traders based there.

Berbers: members of a people living in North Africa, primarily Muslim, living in settled or nomadic tribes between the

Sahara and Mediterranean Sea and between Egypt and the Atlantic Ocean.

binnacle: a built-in housing for a ship's compass.

blighter: a fellow, especially one held in low esteem.

bosun: a ship's officer in charge of supervision and maintenance of the ship and its equipment.

Brobdingnagian: of or relating to a gigantic person or thing; comes from the book *Gulliver's Travels* of 1726 by Jonathan Swift, wherein Gulliver meets the huge inhabitants of Brobdingnag. It is now used in reference to anything huge.

Colt .45: a .45-caliber automatic pistol manufactured by the Colt Firearms Company of Hartford, Connecticut. Colt was founded in 1847 by Samuel Colt (1814–1862), who revolutionized the firearms industry.

Devil's Island: an island in the Caribbean Sea off French Guiana and location of a notorious French penal colony, opened in 1854 and closed in 1946. Used by France, its inmates were everything from political prisoners to the most hardened of thieves and murderers. Conditions were harsh and many prisoners sent there were never seen again. Few convicts ever managed to escape.

djellaba: a long loose hooded garment with full sleeves, worn especially in Muslim countries.

dodger: a canvas or wood screen to provide protection from ocean spray on a ship.

fathom: a unit of length equal to six feet (1.83 meters), used in measuring the depth of water.

Fort-de-France: the capital and largest city of Martinique, on the western coast of the island.

Franzawi: (Arabic) Frenchman.

French Guiana: a French colony of northeast South America on the Atlantic Ocean, established in the nineteenth century and known for its penal colonies (now closed). Cayenne is the capital and the largest city.

gangway: a narrow, movable platform or ramp forming a bridge by which to board or leave a ship.

gendarme: a police officer in any of several European countries, especially a French police officer.

gingham dog and the calico cat: reference to a children's poem called "The Duel" by Eugene Field (1850–1895) about two stuffed toys, a dog made of gingham (a checkered pattern cloth) and a cat made of calico (a floral pattern cloth). The dog and cat in the poem are said to fight all night long until they had eaten each other up and there was nothing left.

G-men: government men; agents of the Federal Bureau of Investigation.

hard-boiled: tough; unsentimental.

hawse: hawse pipe; iron or steel pipe in the stem or bow of a vessel, through which an anchor cable passes.

hein?: (French) eh?

hooker: an older vessel, usually a cargo boat.

knot: a unit of speed, equal to one nautical mile, or about 1.15 miles, per hour.

la Légion: (French) the Legion; the French Foreign Legion.

lay to: to put a ship in a dock or other place of safety.

Legionnaire: a member of the French Foreign Legion, a unique elite unit within the French Army established in 1831. It was created as a unit for foreign volunteers and was primarily used to protect and expand the French colonial empire during the nineteenth century, but has also taken part in all of France's wars with other European powers. It is known to be an elite military unit whose training focuses not only on traditional military skills, but also on the building of a strong *esprit de corps* amongst members. As its men come from different countries with different cultures, this is a widely accepted solution to strengthen them enough to work as a team. Training is often not only physically hard with brutal training methods, but also extremely stressful with high rates of desertion.

Mannlicher: a type of rifle equipped with a manually operated sliding bolt that loads cartridges for firing. Ferdinand Mannlicher, an Austrian engineer and armaments designer, created rifles that were considered reasonably strong and accurate.

Martinique: an island in the eastern Caribbean; administered as an overseas region of France.

mestizo: a racially mixed person, especially in Latin America, of American Indian and European (usually Spanish or Portuguese) ancestry.

metal: mettle; spirited determination.

Monsieur: (French) Mr.

Moorish barb: a desert horse of a breed introduced by the Moors (Muslim people of mixed Berber and Arab descent) that resembles the Arabian horse and is known for speed and endurance.

Moroccan: of Morocco, a country in North Africa. It has a coast on the Atlantic Ocean that reaches past the Strait of Gibraltar into the Mediterranean Sea.

m'sieu: (French) Mr.

old, my: used as a term of cordiality and familiarity.

painter: a rope, usually at the bow, for fastening a boat to a ship, stake, etc.

Paramaribo: the capital and largest city of Dutch Guiana (now Suriname) in northern South America on the Atlantic Ocean.

patois: a regional form of a language, especially of French, differing from the standard, literary form of the language.

put in: to enter a port or harbor, especially for shelter, repairs or provisions.

Qu'est-ce que c'est?: (French) What is that?

reduction gear: a set of gears in an engine used to reduce output speed relative to that of the engine while providing greater turning power.

rhum vieux: (French) aged rum; rum that has aged at least three years.

rudder: a means of steering a boat or ship, usually in the form of a pivoting blade under the water, mounted at the stern and controlled by a wheel or handle.

Scheherazade: the female narrator of *The Arabian Nights*, who during one thousand and one adventurous nights saved her life by entertaining her husband, the king, with stories.

schooner: a fast sailing ship with at least two masts and with sails set lengthwise.

scuppers: openings in the side of a ship at deck level that allow water to run off.

seacocks: valves below the waterline in a ship's hull, used for admitting outside water into some part of the hull.

Shilha: the Berber dialect spoken in the mountains of southern Morocco.

six strength: a wind strength with large waves and foam crests, some spray and winds at 25–31 miles per hour, as classified on the Beaufort scale created in 1805 by Sir Francis Beaufort. The scale ranges from "zero," describing winds of 0–12 miles per hour, to "twelve," describing hurricane-force winds of 73 miles per hour or higher.

slop chest: locker or chest containing a supply of clothing, boots, tobacco and other personal goods for sale to the crew of a ship during a voyage.

Snider: a rifle formerly used in the British service. It was invented by American Jacob Snider in the mid-1800s. The Snider was a breech-loading rifle, derived from its muzzle-loading predecessor called the Enfield.

superstructure: cabins and rooms above the deck of a ship.

telegraph: an apparatus, usually mechanical, for transmitting and receiving orders between the bridge of a ship and the engine room or some other part of the engineering department.

tender: a small boat used to ferry passengers and light cargo between ship and shore.

three sheets to the wind: staggering drunk. This expression refers to a ship whose sheets (ropes, cables or chains used to control the movable corners of a sail) have come loose, causing the sails to flap uncontrolled and the ship to meander at the mercy of the elements, mimicking the unsteady walk of a drunken man.

transom: transom seat; a kind of bench seat, usually with a locker or drawers underneath.

weigh anchor: take up the anchor when ready to sail.

wing: bridge wing; a narrow walkway extending outward from both sides of a pilothouse to the full width of a ship.

L. Ron Hubbard
in the Golden Age
of Pulp Fiction

*In writing an adventure story
a writer has to know that he is adventuring
for a lot of people who cannot.
The writer has to take them here and there
about the globe and show them
excitement and love and realism.
As long as that writer is living the part of an
adventurer when he is hammering
the keys, he is succeeding with his story.*

*Adventuring is a state of mind.
If you adventure through life, you have a
good chance to be a success on paper.*

*Adventure doesn't mean globe-trotting,
exactly, and it doesn't mean great deeds.
Adventuring is like art.
You have to live it to make it real.*

— *L. RON HUBBARD*

L. Ron Hubbard
and American
Pulp Fiction

B ORN March 13, 1911, L. Ron Hubbard lived a life at
least as expansive as the stories with which he enthralled
a hundred million readers through a fifty-year career.

Originally hailing from Tilden, Nebraska, he spent his
formative years in a classically rugged Montana, replete with
the cowpunchers, lawmen and desperadoes who would later
people his Wild West adventures. And lest anyone imagine
those adventures were drawn from vicarious experience, he
was not only breaking broncs at a tender age, he was also
among the few whites ever admitted into Blackfoot society
as a bona fide blood brother. While if only to round out an
otherwise rough and tumble youth, his mother was that rarity
of her time—a thoroughly educated woman—who introduced
her son to the classics of Occidental literature even before
his seventh birthday.

But as any dedicated L. Ron Hubbard reader will attest, his
world extended far beyond Montana. In point of fact, and as the
son of a United States naval officer, by the age of eighteen he
had traveled over a quarter of a million miles. Included therein
were three Pacific crossings to a then still mysterious Asia, where
he ran with the likes of Her British Majesty's agent-in-place

L. Ron Hubbard,
left, at Congressional
Airport, Washington,
DC, 1931, with
members of George
Washington
University flying
club.

for North China, and the last in the line of Royal Magicians from the court of Kublai Khan. For the record, L. Ron Hubbard was also among the first Westerners to gain admittance to forbidden Tibetan monasteries below Manchuria, and his photographs of China's Great Wall long graced American geography texts.

Upon his return to the United States and a hasty completion of his interrupted high school education, the young Ron Hubbard entered George Washington University. There, as fans of his aerial adventures may have heard, he earned his wings as a pioneering barnstormer at the dawn of American aviation. He also earned a place in free-flight record books for the longest sustained flight above Chicago. Moreover, as a roving reporter for *Sportsman Pilot* (featuring his first professionally penned articles), he further helped inspire a generation of pilots who would take America to world airpower.

Immediately beyond his sophomore year, Ron embarked on the first of his famed ethnological expeditions, initially to then untrammeled Caribbean shores (descriptions of which would later fill a whole series of West Indies mystery-thrillers). That the Puerto Rican interior would also figure into the future of Ron Hubbard stories was likewise no accident. For in addition to cultural studies of the island, a 1932–33

LRH expedition is rightly remembered as conducting the first complete mineralogical survey of a Puerto Rico under United States jurisdiction.

There was many another adventure along this vein: As a lifetime member of the famed Explorers Club, L. Ron Hubbard charted North Pacific waters with the first shipboard radio direction finder, and so pioneered a long-range navigation system universally employed until the late twentieth century. While not to put too fine an edge on it, he also held a rare Master Mariner's license to pilot any vessel, of any tonnage in any ocean.

Yet lest we stray too far afield, there is an LRH note at this juncture in his saga, and it reads in part:

"I started out writing for the pulps, writing the best I knew, writing for every mag on the stands, slanting as well as I could."

To which one might add: His earliest submissions date from the

Capt. L. Ron Hubbard in Ketchikan, Alaska, 1940, on his Alaskan Radio Experimental Expedition, the first of three voyages conducted under the Explorers Club flag.

summer of 1934, and included tales drawn from true-to-life Asian adventures, with characters roughly modeled on British/American intelligence operatives he had known in Shanghai. His early Westerns were similarly peppered with details drawn from personal experience. Although therein lay a first hard lesson from the often cruel world of the pulps. His first Westerns were soundly rejected as lacking the authenticity of a Max Brand yarn (a particularly frustrating comment given L. Ron Hubbard's Westerns came straight from his Montana homeland, while Max Brand was a mediocre New York poet named Frederick Schiller Faust, who turned out implausible six-shooter tales from the terrace of an Italian villa).

Nevertheless, and needless to say, L. Ron Hubbard persevered and soon earned a reputation as among the most publishable names in pulp fiction, with a ninety percent placement rate of first-draft manuscripts. He was also among the most prolific, averaging between seventy and a hundred thousand words a month. Hence the rumors that L. Ron Hubbard had redesigned a typewriter for faster keyboard action and pounded out manuscripts on a continuous roll of butcher paper to save the precious seconds it took to insert a single sheet of paper into manual typewriters of the day.

That all L. Ron Hubbard stories did not run beneath said byline is yet another aspect of pulp fiction lore. That is, as publishers periodically rejected manuscripts from top-drawer authors if only to avoid paying top dollar, L. Ron Hubbard and company just as frequently replied with submissions under various pseudonyms. In Ron's case, the

---

A MAN OF MANY NAMES

Between 1934 and 1950, L. Ron Hubbard authored more than fifteen million words of fiction in more than two hundred classic publications. To supply his fans and editors with stories across an array of genres and pulp titles, he adopted fifteen pseudonyms in addition to his already renowned L. Ron Hubbard byline.

Winchester Remington Colt
Lt. Jonathan Daly
Capt. Charles Gordon
Capt. L. Ron Hubbard
Bernard Hubbel
Michael Keith
Rene Lafayette
Legionnaire 148
Legionnaire 14830
Ken Martin
Scott Morgan
Lt. Scott Morgan
Kurt von Rachen
Barry Randolph
Capt. Humbert Reynolds

list included: Rene Lafayette, Captain Charles Gordon, Lt. Scott Morgan and the notorious Kurt von Rachen—supposedly on the lam for a murder rap, while hammering out two-fisted prose in Argentina. The point: While L. Ron Hubbard as Ken Martin spun stories of Southeast Asian intrigue, LRH as Barry Randolph authored tales of

L. Ron Hubbard, circa 1930, at the outset of a literary career that would finally span half a century.

romance on the Western range—which, stretching between a dozen genres is how he came to stand among the two hundred elite authors providing close to a million tales through the glory days of American Pulp Fiction.

In evidence of exactly that, by 1936 L. Ron Hubbard was literally leading pulp fiction's elite as president of New York's American Fiction Guild. Members included a veritable pulp hall of fame: Lester "Doc Savage" Dent, Walter "The Shadow" Gibson, and the legendary Dashiell Hammett—to cite but a few.

Also in evidence of just where L. Ron Hubbard stood within his first two years on the American pulp circuit: By the spring of 1937, he was ensconced in Hollywood, adopting a Caribbean thriller for Columbia Pictures, remembered today as *The Secret of Treasure Island.* Comprising fifteen thirty-minute episodes, the L. Ron Hubbard screenplay led to the most profitable matinée serial in Hollywood history. In accord with Hollywood culture, he was thereafter continually called upon

The 1937 Secret of Treasure Island, *a fifteen-episode serial adapted for the screen by L. Ron Hubbard from his novel,* Murder at Pirate Castle.

to rewrite/doctor scripts—most famously for long-time friend and fellow adventurer Clark Gable.

In the interim—and herein lies another distinctive chapter of the L. Ron Hubbard story—he continually worked to open Pulp Kingdom gates to up-and-coming authors. Or, for that matter, anyone who wished to write. It was a fairly unconventional stance, as markets were already thin and competition razor sharp. But the fact remains, it was an L. Ron Hubbard hallmark that he vehemently lobbied on behalf of young authors—regularly supplying instructional articles to trade journals, guest-lecturing to short story classes at George Washington University and Harvard, and even founding his own creative writing competition. It was established in 1940, dubbed the Golden Pen, and guaranteed winners both New York representation and publication in *Argosy*.

But it was John W. Campbell Jr.'s *Astounding Science Fiction* that finally proved the most memorable LRH vehicle. While every fan of L. Ron Hubbard's galactic epics undoubtedly knows the story, it nonetheless bears repeating: By late 1938, the pulp publishing magnate of Street & Smith was determined to revamp *Astounding Science Fiction* for broader readership. In particular, senior editorial director F. Orlin Tremaine called for stories with a stronger *human element*. When acting editor John W. Campbell balked, preferring his spaceship-driven tales, Tremaine enlisted Hubbard. Hubbard, in turn, replied with the genre's first truly *character-driven* works, wherein heroes are pitted not against bug-eyed monsters but the mystery and majesty of deep space itself—and thus was launched the Golden Age of Science Fiction.

The names alone are enough to quicken the pulse of any science fiction aficionado, including LRH friend and protégé, Robert Heinlein, Isaac Asimov, A. E. van Vogt and Ray Bradbury. Moreover, when coupled with LRH stories of fantasy, we further come to what's rightly been described as the foundation of every modern tale of horror: L. Ron Hubbard's immortal *Fear.* It was rightly proclaimed by Stephen King as one of the very few works to genuinely warrant that overworked term "classic"—as in: *"This is a classic tale of creeping, surreal menace and horror. . . . This is one of the really, really good ones."*

To accommodate the greater body of L. Ron Hubbard fantasies, Street & Smith inaugurated *Unknown*—a classic pulp if there ever was one, and wherein readers were soon thrilling to the likes of *Typewriter in the Sky* and *Slaves of Sleep* of which Frederik Pohl would declare: *"There are bits and pieces from Ron's work that became part of the language in ways that very few other writers managed."*

L. Ron Hubbard, 1948, among fellow science fiction luminaries at the World Science Fiction Convention in Toronto.

And, indeed, at J. W. Campbell Jr.'s insistence, Ron was regularly drawing on themes from the Arabian Nights and so introducing readers to a world of genies, jinn, Aladdin and Sinbad—all of which, of course, continue to float through cultural mythology to this day.

At least as influential in terms of post-apocalypse stories was L. Ron Hubbard's 1940 *Final Blackout*. Generally acclaimed as the finest anti-war novel of the decade and among the ten best works of the genre ever authored—here, too, was a tale that would live on in ways few other writers imagined.

Portland, Oregon, 1943; L. Ron Hubbard, captain of the US Navy subchaser PC 815.

Hence, the later Robert Heinlein verdict: "Final Blackout *is as perfect a piece of science fiction as has ever been written.*"

Like many another who both lived and wrote American pulp adventure, the war proved a tragic end to Ron's sojourn in the pulps. He served with distinction in four theaters and was highly decorated for commanding corvettes in the North Pacific. He was also grievously wounded in combat, lost many a close friend and colleague and thus resolved to say farewell to pulp fiction and devote himself to what it had supported these many years—namely, his serious research.

But in no way was the LRH literary saga at an end, for as he wrote some thirty years later, in 1980:

"Recently there came a period when I had little to do. This was novel in a life so crammed with busy years, and I decided to amuse myself by writing a novel that was pure *science fiction."*

That work was *Battlefield Earth: A Saga of the Year 3000*. It was an immediate *New York Times* bestseller and, in fact, the first international science fiction blockbuster in decades. It was not, however, L. Ron Hubbard's magnum opus, as that distinction is generally reserved for his next and final work: The 1.2 million word *Mission Earth*.

> **Final Blackout**
> *is as perfect a piece of science fiction as has ever been written.*
>
> —Robert Heinlein

How he managed those 1.2 million words in just over twelve months is yet another piece of the L. Ron Hubbard legend. But the fact remains, he did indeed author a ten-volume *dekalogy* that lives in publishing history for the fact that each and every volume of the series was also a *New York Times* bestseller.

Moreover, as subsequent generations discovered L. Ron Hubbard through republished works and novelizations of his screenplays, the mere fact of his name on a cover signaled an international bestseller. . . . Until, to date, sales of his works exceed hundreds of millions, and he otherwise remains among the most enduring and widely read authors in literary history. Although as a final word on the tales of L. Ron Hubbard, perhaps it's enough to simply reiterate what editors told readers in the glory days of American Pulp Fiction:

He writes the way he does, brothers, because he's been there, seen it and done it!

THE STORIES FROM THE GOLDEN AGE

Your ticket to adventure starts here with the Stories from
the Golden Age collection by master storyteller L. Ron Hubbard.
These gripping tales are set in a kaleidoscope of exotic locales and brim
with fascinating characters, including some of the
most vile villains, dangerous dames and brazen heroes
you'll ever get to meet.

The entire collection of over one hundred and fifty stories is being
released in a series of eighty books and audiobooks.
For an up-to-date listing of available titles,
go to www.goldenagestories.com.

AIR ADVENTURE

Arctic Wings	*Man-Killers of the Air*
The Battling Pilot	*On Blazing Wings*
Boomerang Bomber	*Red Death Over China*
The Crate Killer	*Sabotage in the Sky*
The Dive Bomber	*Sky Birds Dare!*
Forbidden Gold	*The Sky-Crasher*
Hurtling Wings	*Trouble on His Wings*
The Lieutenant Takes the Sky	*Wings Over Ethiopia*

FAR-FLUNG ADVENTURE

The Adventure of "X"
All Frontiers Are Jealous
The Barbarians
The Black Sultan
Black Towers to Danger
The Bold Dare All
Buckley Plays a Hunch
The Cossack
Destiny's Drum
Escape for Three
Fifty-Fifty O'Brien
The Headhunters
Hell's Legionnaire
He Walked to War
Hostage to Death

Hurricane
The Iron Duke
Machine Gun 21,000
Medals for Mahoney
Price of a Hat
Red Sand
The Sky Devil
The Small Boss of Nunaloha
The Squad That Never Came Back
Starch and Stripes
Tomb of the Ten Thousand Dead
Trick Soldier
While Bugles Blow!
Yukon Madness

SEA ADVENTURE

Cargo of Coffins
The Drowned City
False Cargo
Grounded
Loot of the Shanung
Mister Tidwell, Gunner

The Phantom Patrol
Sea Fangs
Submarine
Twenty Fathoms Down
Under the Black Ensign

TALES FROM THE ORIENT

MYSTERY

119

FANTASY

SCIENCE FICTION

WESTERN